CORPUS
CHRISTI

For Jessica —

Read and memorize!

And good luck with
your own work —
see you in print —

Billy

CORPUS CHRISTI

Stories

Bret Anthony Johnston

RANDOM HOUSE

NEW YORK

Copyright © 2004 by Bret Anthony Johnston

All rights reserved under International and Pan-American Copyright
Conventions. Published in the United States by Random House,
an imprint of The Random House Publishing Group, a division
of Random House, Inc., New York, and simultaneously in Canada
by Random House of Canada Limited, Toronto.

RANDOM HOUSE and colophon are registered trademarks
of Random House, Inc.

These stories originally appeared in the following publications:
"Waterwalkers": *Open City,* January 2004, and *Stories from the Blue Moon
Café III,* August 2004; "I See Something You Don't See": *Crazyhorse,* Spring
2003 (published as "How Much Brighter the Stars"); "In the Tall Grass":
Shenandoah, Fall 2000; "Outside the Toy Store": *Faultline,* Spring 2001;
"Corpus Christi": *New Stories from the South: The Year's Best, 2003,* July 2003,
and *Black Warrior Review,* Fall 2002 (published as "Corpus"); "The Widow":
New Stories from the South: The Year's Best, 2004, July 2004, and *New England
Review,* Spring 2003; "Two Liars": *Scribner's Best of the Fiction Workshops
1999,* April 1999, and *Clackamas Literary Review,* Fall 1998 (published as
"Smoke"); "Anything That Floats": *The Paris Review,* Winter 2004; "Birds of
Paradise": *Southwest Review,* Winter 2001; "Buy for Me the Rain":
The Greensboro Review, Fall 2002 (published as "Condolences").

Library of Congress Cataloging-in-Publication Data
Johnston, Bret Anthony.
Corpus Christi : stories / Bret Anthony Johnston.
p. cm.
ISBN 1-4000-6211-X
1. Corpus Christi (Tex.)—Fiction. I. Title.
PS3610.O384C67 2004
813'.54—dc22   2003069315

Printed in the United States of America on acid-free paper
Random House website address: www.atrandom.com
2 4 6 8 9 7 5 3 1
First Edition

Book design by Victoria Wong

For Jennifer, my ideal reader

Acknowledgments

I'M GRATEFUL TO MY TEACHERS WHO BECAME friends and to my friends who've taught me: Ethan Canin. Frank Conroy. Marilynne Robinson. Connie Brothers. Deb West. Jan Z. Amy Margolis. Josh Emmons. Dan Pope. Joe Wilson, Cheryl Pfoff. Mike Anzaldua. Vanessa Jackson. Steven Bauer. Eric Goodman. Kay Sloan. Constance Pierce. Joseph Martinez. Ivan Pena. Michelle Harper. Gary and Lizz Cosgrove. Anne Greene. Katie Hanson. John Smolens. Tom Bligh. Curtis Sittenfeld. Serenity Gerbman and the Southern Festival of Books. Shannon Ravenel, Chelcy Boyer, and especially Kathy "Special K" Pories. This book, quite literally, would not exist without the countless wise and generous readings of Jonathan Liebson.

Thank you, ever so much, to the editors who supported these stories: David Mitchell Goldberg. Shannon Ravenel (again). Joanna Yas and Elizabeth Schmidt. C. Michael Curtis. Jodee Rubins and Stephen Donadio. Jim Clark. Willard

Spiegelman. Tim Schell. Natalie Danford, John Kulka, and Sherman Alexie. Bret Lott. R. T. Smith. Elizabeth Gaffney. Sonny Brewer.

At Random House, I'm deeply indebted to the tireless Stephanie Higgs, Tim Farrell, Steve Messina, and Jynne "the Viking" Martin. Everyone who's had the luxury of working with Dan Menaker marvels at how he does all that he does, and his deft hand made these stories better versions of themselves. For that, and for all that he's taught me, I cannot thank him enough.

Likewise, the unwavering enthusiasm of the Collins McCormick Literary Agency is beyond compare. O brave new world that has such an agent as Nina Collins in it.

Bill, my brother, deserves a record deal for all he's given me.

Finally, I know of no words to properly thank my parents, but this book is the closest I've come so far. I'll keep trying.

Contents

CORPUS
CHRISTI

Waterwalkers

As hurricane Alicia drifted north-northwest up the Gulf Coast from Veracruz, Mexico, Sonny Atwill stood outside McCoy's Lumber hanging NO PLYWOOD signs in the windows. A gray, blurring rain blew over the parking lot, diffusing the headlights of cars waiting for empty spaces. Horns blared and bleated. In addition to the plywood being gone, the store was low on batteries, masking tape, flashlights, kerosene lanterns, bottled water, sandbags and propane. Originally the Hurricane Center had predicted that Baffin Bay, Texas, would bear the brunt, but revised reports had it heading for Corpus Christi, making landfall that evening. Sonny believed the storm would veer south, go in around Laredo; he'd projected its course with a grease pencil on his laminated hurricane map.

When he came back inside the store, a woman was sitting at the bottom of a rolling ladder in the cabinet fixtures aisle, crying. She had her face cupped in her hands. He thought to sidestep the hassle and let someone else explain that the store was sold out of everything she would need. This was what he'd learned over the years: Stay out of it. He was fifty-nine, retired from Coastal Oil Refinery, working ten hours a week at McCoy's because his doctor wanted him to exercise. Usually he was off on Friday, but when the shipment had unexpectedly arrived last night, the manager had ponied up ten sheets of plywood for Sonny himself to use, plus regular pay, if he would clock in this morning. The woman kept her back to him as she stood. *Leave her be,* he thought once more—*let the husband come.* Yet he was drawn to her, reluctantly compelled to suggest other lumberyards and offer the possibility that the storm would spare them. Then, hurriedly, she turned and their eyes met. "Sonny," she said. He took a single unintentional step backward, emptied and suspended.

"My sister," Nora finally said, but then she fell to weeping again. She wore a white scoop neck blouse, faded jeans. In twelve years, she'd lost ten, maybe twenty pounds; her ring finger was naked. Sonny knelt beside her, vaguely hearing the announcement that McCoy's would close in fifteen minutes. Whenever his son had been excited, he'd said butterflies were tickling his palms, and now that seemed the perfect description for the way Sonny felt. Nora wiped her eyes and said, "My sister has huge windows."

FOR YEARS, HE HAD THROWN HURRICANE PARTIES. Named storms hit four and five times a season, and he would clean out the garage and fry flounder and invite people from the oil refinery. They sat in frayed lawn chairs and drank Schlitz, watching a storm's edge cut off the horizon like a charcoal sheet and playing cards—Mexican Sweat, Texas Hold'em, Stud—until the wind howled. Then they slipped into plastic ponchos and danced. He'd mounted a battery-powered radio over the workbench (to hear the Oilers lose while he fiddled with the lawn mower), and they listened to tapes—Anne Murray, George Jones, Johnny Rodriguez. Once, a Kmart sign had cartwheeled through the yard. A man from the refinery had brought Janice Steele to the party, then she'd borrowed Sonny's phone to call her sister and invite her. When the storm broke up and the others left, Nora stayed.

That was 1972, the year he was named supervisor of an eight-man crew. He was thirty-one, Nora twenty-six. She shelved books at the library while attending the community college at night; she aimed to earn her teaching certificate. They had been together a few months when he bought the house he'd been renting on Shamrock Street. She moved in, filling the rooms with her expensive, honeyed shampoos, hanging ivies and matted photographs. Each Sunday they drove to an open-air restaurant on the Laguna Madre and ate baskets of shrimp and hush puppies. One night she said, *"Take all away from me, but leave me Ecstasy."*

Her voice was so low and cool that his heart stuttered. He asked, "Does that mean you want another beer?"

"It means I want you to marry me."

The wind lifted a corner of the red-checked tablecloth, raising it gently from the slatted table then dropping it again;

waves sloshed heavily against pylons; the smell of batter and fish and salt-splashed cedar; the divine heat in his chest, like a ray of light refracted in a jewel.

THE WEATHER SLACKED OFF AFTER MCCOY'S CLOSED. Sonny followed Nora to her sister's on Del Mar Street. The talk-radio station he liked was overrun with storm coverage: Authorities had taken down traffic lights around the harbor and were evacuating boats from the bay; Alicia's sustained winds topped 115 miles per hour; the Navy was tying down vessels in mooring systems and deploying others to sea; ferry service had been halted, and soon rising tides would close off Padre and Mustang Islands. Residents were advised to bring in pets, stock up on canned goods, caulk bathtub drains and fill the tubs with water.

She drove slowly, her brake lights blinking like Morse code. Traffic was bottlenecked at the freeway; shoe-polished windshields read HELP US JESUS and GO AWAY ALICIA! The city's south side was flooding. Corpus seemed transformed, like a dream version of itself from which a somnolent atmosphere had been cast off; wind made street signs tremble. What he felt behind the wheel was a long-dormant vulnerability. When he had offered Nora his plywood—it lay in his truck bed, under the camper—she had accepted by saying, "So here we go again."

Del Mar was a wide, palm-lined street, a quarter mile from the bay. The house was a five-bedroom with a French garden and greenhouse that Sonny had helped build; Janice grew orchids. She was summering in Italy—"with some Guido," as Nora put it—so she was house-sitting. Janice was an attorney who had never married, and whenever Sonny had passed the house in intervening years, he thought a place so large would depress you to live alone in. Years before, he'd moved into an all-utilities-paid duplex and put the money from the Shamrock house in mutual funds. He wondered if Nora had avoided Shamrock since she'd been back, or if she'd seen the newly painted trim, the garden trellis and oak saplings, the lush elephant ears she'd never been able to grow.

He backed into the gravel driveway, doubting he could finish boarding up before the sky opened again. The house looked larger, the windows higher. Nora had calmed; maybe she'd taken a tranquilizer. She greeted him now with a familiar distractedness, an improbable air of casual lightness, as if she'd just returned from shopping and needed to get some milk into the icebox. Her rejuvenation disappointed him, as did how quickly she disappeared inside. He'd hoped she might ask his opinion on Alicia, maybe even tear up again. He buckled his tool belt and switched out the bit in the cordless drill he'd borrowed from McCoy's. He hoisted each sheet of plywood onto his thigh, held it to the house with his left hand, then screwed the sides, corners, top, bottom. Twice the drill twisted and caught the flesh between his thumb and finger. He took breathers between gusts and each breath felt like a spear in his ribs. Hammers banged on nearby streets;

a circular saw whined; a woman started calling for a pet named Scooter. Sonny tried not to stomp the snapdragons and budding hydrangeas, but that proved impossible.

And not unexpectedly he heard Max—the memory of his voice still strong and clear, like a good radio signal. They could've been sitting in the Shamrock kitchen, the boy's elbows propped on the newly laid-in countertop, an evening when they studied for the merit badge test. He was eight, fawn-skinned and sharp-cheeked like Nora, fascinated by windmills and in the habit of climbing into their bed after they'd gone to sleep. Recently he'd been prone to lying, was in fact currently grounded for it. The restriction opened up the after-supper hours to tie knots and practice splinting broken limbs and to review the history of the Karankawa Indians, the first inhabitants of South Texas: Members of the tribe stood over six feet tall, wore no clothes and were known cannibals; they slept on dried palms, tattooed themselves from head to foot and smeared the inside of their leaky pottery with asphaltum that had washed ashore. Sonny asked Max for the translation of the tribe's name.

The boy filled his cheeks with air, pouting, stalling, then he exhaled. He said, "Waterwalkers."

"No," Sonny said. "Dog-raisers."

"But also Waterwalkers," he said. "They can also be called Waterwalkers."

At Janice's, the drill twisted again, and Nora said, "Guess you didn't need help."

Her voice made him feel cornered, ashamed. She had changed into a loose sweater, a fisherman's hat and old sneakers. He'd liked her in the scoop neck and wished she hadn't taken it off, though maybe that was precisely why she had.

"Small potatoes," he said. It was not something he'd said before, and he had no idea where it had come from. His heart was still pumping hard. His face felt raddled, his mind dull; he regretted that he hadn't shaved before work, that he'd worn such a wrinkled shirt.

"That one would've been a bugger," he said.

The front of the two-story house across the street was more glass than brick.

"Architects," she said. "Remember? The Christmas party."

"That's all a blur for me. The old noggin mixes things up lately."

"I doubt that. But if you're serious, at least you held out longer than I did."

He returned to the plywood, cranking down already tight screws. He wanted to shy away from solemn conversations.

"The first storm of the season, in August, and it just turned Category Four."

"Welcome home," he said, but the words sounded laden, riven with an inappropriate, boastful enthusiasm. He said, "We'll get some wind, but she'll spare us. There'll be a good haul of shrimp behind the weather."

"Alicia. They always pick pretty names for the first ones."

She had believed this since he'd known her and had always

cited the first storms—Ayla, Antonio, Amelia—to evidence her point. That she still observed it pleased him.

A kettle whistled inside Janice's kitchen, a room where he'd carved beef for holidays, Super Bowls, the funeral. The night of the architects' party, he'd crossed the street for more gin and spied Janice bent over the butcher-block table, an architect biting her neck and groping her breasts.

A stiff breeze riffled the palms near the street. Across Ocean Drive, the sky faded downward by degrees, violet to lavender to oyster silver, until at last it softened into a seam of sallow light on the horizon.

Nora said, "I boiled water. I thought some tea might take our mind off things."

ONCE, HE'D SEEN JANICE IN THE CLUBHOUSE OF Oso Municipal Golf Course. She'd played nine holes with partners from the law firm and sat at the bar drinking screwdrivers. Raking her fingers through her hair and leaning back to expel plumes of smoke, she resembled Nora. The men around her burst into laughter at a joke she made while fishing through her purse. One of them said, "That *is* a hole in one," as she started for the door. Sonny thought he'd escaped her, then she shuffled over to his booth. He was finishing a Reuben—gratis, like his rounds, because he maintained the course's carts and sprinklers on weekends—and he was reading about Karankawas.

He said, "These fellas used to slather themselves with mud and shark grease."

"Injun Old Spice," said Janice. Her eyes were red-rimmed, her lips slow.

"Repelled mosquitoes," he said. "They also talked—communicated—with their mouths closed."

"So do those lawyers." She pointed at them with her chin.

Her hair was cropped, highlighted white and gold. Not a style Nora would ever wear, so having confused the resemblance irritated him. He'd intended to carry on about the Karankawas, explain how they would tie lanterns to a mule's neck and lead it in circles on darkened beaches to attract vessels at sea. A captain would read the distant light as a buoy and steer his boat toward the harbor he assumed it marked. By the time he realized his mistake, he'd have struck the outer sandbar and the naked Indians would emerge with spears. But now all of that seemed trivial and Sonny explained nothing. He heard himself say, "I haven't gotten a word in a while."

Immediately he wished he'd not mentioned Nora, and at the same time he wanted Janice to spill what she knew. For a while, he'd received postcards and late-night weepy calls. He told her that he'd not contested when Coastal proposed the early retirement; she said she missed hearing surf reports on the radio, missed good chalupas. He resisted the urge to call her Honey or Love or No-No. They never spoke of Max. Then the communications dwindled, and a blankness set in, as if not reporting his actions to Nora, not even *planning* to report them, stripped them of any significance. She had lived in Michigan, Arizona, Nebraska and North Dakota, locales untouched by the ocean, and he knew she would never return to Corpus. His days were incurably wide and ponderous, and at night he fought phantom jealousies of other men.

After the retirement, he'd moved through life like a fugitive, trepidatious and worried that he would meet someone from the old times. If he glimpsed an acquaintance in the supermarket, he lingered in a far-off aisle or abandoned a full cart of groceries and fled to his truck. If someone caught him, at McCoy's or Oso or a pre-dawn bait stand, his veins surged with dreadful eagerness. Those mundane encounters left him utterly unsure of his identity. No longer a father, no longer a husband. And though he felt on the verge of some old, indolent connection—maybe they felt that, too—he'd erected such sturdy walls, perfected such inconspicuous deflections that the conversations passed without even the slightest revelation. The men told him about the refinery hub, which plants were producing more barrels per day, who had passed on and who was stealing compressors to sell out of his garage; they avoided mention of families. Sonny spoke of golf and fishing; he told them he was living the life he'd always worked for.

At the clubhouse Janice had run her tongue between her teeth and lips. She was older than Nora by five years, but people had always thought her younger.

"She's working at a bakery. In Ann Arbor," she said. "But that's yesterday's sad tune. I want to hear about good old Sonny."

He said, "I put one foot in front of the other, like a good soldier."

"And the ladies? Still need a stick to keep them away?"

He washed down the last of his Reuben and wiped his mouth with a napkin. Lois Whipple was at her house, slow-cooking a roast, vacuuming, and curling her hair for tonight. He'd been seeing her for two months, but already he smelled the relationship rotting on the vine.

"No," he said. "Mostly they stay away on their own."

That same afternoon his shoulder numbed. On the sixth green, he recognized the tingling in his fingers and sharp punches in his chest with an almost grateful, razorlike clarity. In his mind was the image of a fist squeezing an aorta, of a child clenching a water balloon, dreading and courting the moment it bursts. He replaced his putter, sat down and waited.

GUSTS STARTED BREAKING BRANCHES OFF TREES, Del Mar was pooling. Tallow leaves eddied in tight circles above the gutters. No doubt boats had been pulled from the marina, trailered into parking lots and vacated streets. An early, slatey dusk descended. If Sonny waited much longer, he'd be marooned through the storm.

"I never got my degree," Nora said cheerfully. "Never transferred my credits. I just enrolled willy-nilly."

They sat at the butcher-block table, opposite each other on wicker stools. She had brought in Janice's grill, the red-wood patio furniture and potted plants—azaleas, macho ferns, a bromeliad. The grill smelled of sodden ash. Six jugs of water sat on the counter, beside a new fire extinguisher.

"Nursing classes mostly," she said. Her eyes went to the abrasions on his thumb, which immediately started throbbing. "We're not wired to remember what hurts us. Our bodies have no memory for pain."

Then she winked. "Biology 101."

"You'd make a keen nurse. Or *will* make. You'll finish soon enough." Then because he couldn't stop himself, he added, "The college just expanded its nursing program here."

"The hospital was the first place I went when I got back. Isn't that typical? The place still smells the same. What did we used to say?"

"Iodine and clover."

"And that hideous mural, Jesus and the Jackass."

A clap of thunder rattled the windows. Nora had always closed her eyes during heavy thunder, as if it saddened her. Opening them, she looked embarrassed. He thought she might be wearing contacts; maybe her vision had deteriorated over the years. How did he look to her now? Had Janice described him from Oso? As a shell, a ghost, a man who'd lost his religion? Or did she afford him that cruelest kindness—*he's holding up fine.* Nora had coped with the events one way and he'd done it another. While he burrowed, she fled.

Yet here they were. The wind straining against the house, rain like pebbles on the plywood. Holding her gaze was impossible, but he stole glances. With one, he noticed the silken line of her neck; with another, the cleft of her lips; another, the creases on her knuckles. Over the years her speech had hastened, her words had acquired the occasional unfamiliar diphthong—she pronounced "about" like a Canadian now. He stayed guarded, flexed against whatever else had changed, ready to absorb how her presence would dissolve his memories, like water on sugar. Still, an anticipation buoyed him. He liked being in the room with her.

A flow of memory rushed just beneath the waking world, like a frozen-over stream; if he wanted, he could punch through the ice and let the current drag him under. Max had stayed here once, sometimes twice, a month, and his aunt ordered pizza, rented movies Nora wouldn't allow at home. He'd always adored Janice, behaved best for her. She had opened her house after the funeral—men and women from the refinery had crowded the stark halls. Many of the artifacts Sonny had discussed with relieving, unprecedented thoroughness still lined Janice's shelves—a framed scrimshaw and wooden giraffe from Kenya, an antique clock from Paris, a bronze statuette from Athens. Commanding one wall was an enormous chiaroscuro of a policeman studying his reflection in a parking meter: Max's favorite.

Nora had started talking about the hurricane again. Sonny said, "I think she'll miss us."

She smiled, then peered into her mug. "You're that same man."

"Same old Sonny."

"Still chasing storms on your little map?" She laughed a small, breathless laugh. A chinaberry's soaked limbs whipped the house, a metal trash can rolled across the street. He paced to the front door, daring himself to imagine a more unlikely, more longed-for night. *What else,* he wondered, *do you remember? What else do you want to know?* Probably she wondered if he still searched out information on the Karankawas, but she kept such questions to herself. Had they been in his duplex, the various Karankawa books stacked in his breakfast nook and around his bed would have prickled his flesh with shame. She stood behind him briefly, touched his shoulder like a woman in a crowd, then returned to the kitchen. Soupy brown water was inching up the yard. His truck, reversed in, was up to its headlights. The weight of her hand lingered, an imprint in drying cement.

NORA HADN'T WANTED MAX TO GO TO CAMP Karankawa; he'd never been away from home for anything close to a week, and a tropical storm was brewing in the Gulf. Meteorologists predicted it would turn and head out into the ocean, but she had undertaken a benign, halfhearted campaign to discourage the trip. ("You could go next year," she said. "You'll be older.") Still, she allowed herself to be convinced that if other scouts were going, if the camp opened despite the weather, then he should go, too. He wanted his merit badge, and he'd been grounded for the last week, so the trip must have seemed a beacon. *He's just at Janice's,* she began telling herself, trying to dismantle his absence into manageable increments. But nothing—not work or cleaning or sleep or conversation—could fill the void; nothing could deliver the nights swiftly enough. She tried distracting herself, her mind and body—restaurants with tasseled menus, candlelit baths, ice cream, letter writing, aerobics. Most of the ideas paled, though, and those that didn't—soaking baths and mint chocolate chip—invigorated rather than relaxed her. Both letters she wrote were to Max.

So she felt relieved and vindicated, Sonny had described her as "plucky," when three days later Max called for them to fetch him. His stomach hurt; he didn't like the beds; mosquitoes bit him at night; he'd pulled a deer tick from his shoulder. The Scoutmaster said Max had a slight fever, but mostly his interest in the camp seemed to have waned after he'd earned his Karankawa patch. Then the homecoming became a double relief because the storm—now Hurricane Fay—had stalled, organized, and was churning back toward the coast. Forecasts anticipated that storm surges would bring tides fifteen feet higher than normal; rain up to an inch every hour. She'd told herself not to throw a fit, not to demand that they drive up and abscond with their embarrassed son, but now that he wanted to come home, she knew she'd been right all along.

Or so Sonny had imagined.

The doctors diagnosed the boy with a flu that was making the rounds; Nora had taken him the day after his return. Sonny intended to meet them there, but a fire had started in the heater of the refinery's No. 4 platformer, then the boss ordered a weekend shutdown because of Fay. When Sonny arrived home that afternoon, Max said, "They didn't give me a shot." And Sonny said, "No? Well, we'll have to go back."

That night, the wind squalled. Max was asleep on the couch, his fever rising with the evening. Now that he was home, Nora wanted, ironically, inappropriately, to make love. She liked sex during storms, always had, but Sonny also knew that Max's being back had returned Nora to herself, and whole again, her body was yearning. And didn't being parents sweeten intimacy anyway? Didn't their lovemaking benefit from the pleasure of escaping accumulated responsibility? Rain in her hair, vodka on her lips, the lovely, briny smell of her sweaty neck, they were nearing that moment when they would forget mortgages and storms and summer colds for a few seconds, the moment when they'd be brilliantly freed from their senses, but she paused and said she wanted to move the boy into his room. "Stay here," she said, the words slow as honey.

What a time for Sonny to recall the raffle tickets: Max wears a dress shirt, creased slacks, loafers that blister his ankles—church clothes. White sunlight dapples the street, a thick wind stirs leaves as he walks; maybe he rehearses his speech. He carries a notebook to record the donations and raps on neighbors' doors. The pitch is that someone's name will be drawn at the end of the fund drive—Frasier Elementary needs money for a new gymnasium, playground equipment, fish tanks and fish—and the winner and two guests will fly, with the top-selling student, to AstroWorld in Houston. He relays the information with the eager, distracted seriousness of a boy whose feet do not yet touch the linoleum under the chair. He accepts cookies and Cokes, kisses on the cheek and handshakes along with the cash; he does not accept checks. He wads the money in his pocket, then proceeds down the block, trying to meet his goal before his father gets home for supper.

What did Nora's screaming sound like as Sonny waited in their bed—how to describe that voice that ripped through the reverie and made his heart knot and turn over in his chest? A barbed, hoarse gasping, like a woman being choked? A wounded wild animal? Are there no words for such afflicted noise?

Max wouldn't wake. In Sonny's memory, time had warped; by the moment he'd kneeled beside the boy, his mind processing the limp arms, the awful surprising weight of an unmuscled, unconscious child, Nora had already been told that ambulances were caught in the weather. She argued irrationally, or hyperrationally, with the dispatcher, but Sonny had slipped into chinos and bolted outside to start the truck, struggling to shut out the sudden overpowering fear that it wouldn't crank. Despite himself, he noticed the mailbox gaping open; a cedar plank in the fence had sunk inches below the rest; their welcome mat floated down the street. There was the consideration of whether to cover Max with something— a garbage bag?—to shield him from the rain, then the decision instead to take a towel and pat him dry in the truck. After Nora situated herself in the passenger seat, he scooped Max from the couch, keeping him swaddled in the blue afghan, and cradled him out into the storm. Ducking outside, Sonny thought: *Breathing, he's breathing.* He did not think to put on his shoes.

A constant sluice of water, the harsh, labored squeak of worn-down wipers. Wind slammed the truck like waves. Nora talked: *Daddy's getting us there.* His foot slipped from the accelerator, his forearms and wrists burned from fighting the steering wheel, water dripped from his hair into his eyes, mouth. *Are you cold? Want more blanket?* The wiper blades wouldn't clear fast enough, each sheet of water replaced by another. He drove in second gear, shifted to third, then back to second. Rain skidded over the pavement, made it appear clean, soft. *Pretend we're on a boat, a ferry.* The engine bogging, bogging, almost choking out under the water. *Remember the ferry? The jumping fish? Remember the Flippers? Sure you do.* He deliberated everything at once; what to do if the engine quits; which streets to take; alternate routes if necessary; what to tell the doctor; in what order. *You're the good one. You're okay. We love you. I'm sorry. I'm sorry.*

Had he opened his eyes? Nora said she thought he had for a second, but she'd turned away, believing they'd missed a turn. Max's face seemed trapped in the glow of streetlamps— a jaundiced gray. They hit deep, hidden puddles and new potholes that jarred the truck and bounced each of them hard on the bench seat. Sonny wanted to slow down, wanted to speed up. Each minute squeezed in around them; they were at the bottom of a well, losing oxygen. Palm trees bowed. The hospital seemed impossibly far; each intersection left him panicked, sick with indecision. Though he retraced their course in his mind and found no mistake, he convinced himself he had taken a wrong turn. The city looked foreign, a maze of

Möbius streets that disappeared behind the truck and led nowhere. He had no idea where he was, where he'd taken his fraught, desperate family, but just as he started to confess, the hospital towers came into view, each distant window ablaze with a promising amber light.

THE OPPORTUNITY TO LEAVE JANICE'S PASSED LIKE a secret. Curtains of rain slapped the north side of the house; the metal garbage can clattered at the top of a driveway; wind slipped between the plywood and the windows, whistling, threatening to pry them apart.

She remembered the hurricane parties differently. No radio, no dancing in the garage, no lawn chairs or slickers. She placed the same friends not in the garage but around the kitchen table, playing dominoes. She had come *with* Janice, not after. A sign *had* sailed across the yard, but she recalled it coming from a nearby gas station—called Kum and Go— not Kmart across town. She told him this sitting in the front room, on a sofa upholstered in Italian silk. Waves of uneasiness rolled over Sonny; he fought back discouragement, a stubborn disbelief. For years he'd thought—fantasized, really—of meeting her again, of happening upon her in an airport or catching her eye in a dark restaurant. He heard himself deliver beautifully aged, devastating orations. He'd had nightmares, too; in one, he stood beside her bathtub and threw a plugged-in television into the water and watched her convulse. Now his words got tangled before he spoke them, his thoughts jettisoned down regrettable tangents.

"I should admit I remarried," she said. "A groundskeeper at a cemetery. I was snapping pictures of headstones for a photography class. He was pulling weeds and called me maudlin."

"I needed that word for a crossword puzzle last Sunday," he said. This was true, but more than anything, he wanted not to hear about this man. He checked her fingers again, expecting a ring to have appeared. Nor did he want to tell about the women he'd dated—a divorced waitress, a pacemaker programmer, a veterinary technician—each more familiar than the last, each another version of the same woman.

Nora said, "We've not spoken in two years, the groundskeeper and I. He believes I used him. His term is 'emotional tampon.'"

She laughed, then he did.

Outside, the wind picked up the garbage can and hurled it against Janice's garage door. They both startled at the sound, then recovered, as if someone had unexpectedly entered and left the room. She said, "Still think it's going to miss us?"

A gentle lilt had crept into her voice, a beseeching tone fringed with playfulness, as though this would become their private joke.

SONNY HAD TAKEN SOLACE IN THE COMPLETENESS of her grief. Her devastation reassured him; he thought, *This makes sense.* She cried and wailed, accepted sympathy and acted alternately hostile and distracted. Then once the obligations were completed, family and friends delivered back to their jobs and homes, she locked herself in Max's room and refused to leave.

He set trays of food outside the door—she wouldn't retrieve them until he showed himself through Max's back window. When the phone rang, she picked up the extension in the room; she used his bathroom, dried herself with his towels, squeezed into his T-shirts. She detailed these things through the door—the wood still plastered with superhero decals and postcards from Janice's travels—while Sonny waited for all of this to end, trusting that something would snap and they'd be liberated from such desolation. But sustaining her became his new project. Her despair so steeled him that he was afraid to upset that balance, and he savored the comfort of again counting on something. The worst feeling, far worse than he could have anticipated, was that tending to her distracted him from Max's absence, that he toiled to sustain her because he'd failed their son; in his darkest moments, he accused himself of employing her hopelessness to pull himself out of the sludge. Or he believed, as never before, that people incurred punishments of the soul.

On the third day she said, "I found a notebook under his bed." Then, after a moment: "He had a little girlfriend. Janie Palmer. She has a pony named Sprinkles."

He knew her immediately. "Blonde. From the assembly."

"Right."

He imagined Nora clutching the notebook against her breasts, gazing up to recall Janie Palmer beside Max, swaying and singing "Home on the Range." He'd worn a cowboy vest fashioned from a paper bag, decorated with crayon zigzags and a tinfoil sheriff's star. He was pigeon-toed and off-key and so beautiful Sonny had to squeeze his eyes closed.

Nora said, "She's a looker! Our little heartbreaker."

And what became clear hearing her voice, bubbling and proud and hopeful for that which would never be, was that he had already lost her. When they had heard the word *meningitis*—they were standing before the hospital's surreal, childlike mural of Christ feeding a donkey on a plain of blond sand—Sonny sensed that a grotesque race had begun and that he was suddenly responsible for their outrunning a catastrophe. A thing like this either bound people together or drove them apart, but now he knew she was gone. Maybe he'd leave lunch outside her door—already it had become *her* door, *her* room—and she'd never answer; maybe tomorrow he'd wake to find her car and clothes gone; maybe in an hour she'd waltz out and they would live together another ten years without exchanging an unkind or meaningful word; maybe she'd cinch Max's paisley tie around her neck and kick his desk chair out from under her.

"Hungry?" he asked.

"Ravenous," she said, still bright. "Is there more cereal?"

"For supper?"

"Doesn't it sound delicious? I have a real taste for sugar lately."

In the kitchen he mashed enough sleeping pills to knock her out and sifted them into the bowl. Within the hour he lifted the door off its hinges, loaded her into the truck, and returned to the hospital.

HE TRIED BRINGING HER BACK, WITH KINDNESS AND romance, with promises and memories and plans and pleas, but she always seemed just beyond reach. Nora seemed to think he wanted her to recover—wanted *them* to recover—and that galled her. But he'd abandoned that dream as he'd abandoned the refinery; when he left for work, he drove to the National Seashore and passed the hours among the mud flats and saltwater marshes. When he returned in the evenings, still under the pretense of a completed shift, she ranted and collapsed, threw accusations and insults and skillets, while all along he was becoming too severe in an unanswerable resistance. No, recovery was not what he wanted; he wanted them to go down together—man, woman, child. But life at home lurched and creaked; love turned into a crossthreaded bolt. He proposed moving from Corpus, and finally that's what she did, alone. The divorce was swift; she wanted nothing except for the marriage to end.

He carted their furniture and housewares, the clothes she'd left and even a few of Max's long-discarded toys onto the lawn and sold them to neighbors and strangers. (After the first plastic tractor sold, he rescued the other toys.) When only piles of blouses and skirts lay on the lawn, he sold the lot for eight dollars. Crystal and antiques went to an auction, yielding more than he'd expected; he sold the Shamrock house after a year in the duplex. Then a deadly void opened—a steep, widening channel across which he still heard her voice and saw her visage—but trying to ford the space would kill him sure as cancer. Days came when he could feel Nora's presence, as if she'd arrived in Corpus for a visit but hadn't yet called. Sometimes he heard her saying his name, others he glimpsed her zipping by in traffic. Once he saw her at the cemetery, kneeling beside the headstone. He made his way to her, thinking how fittingly peculiar the scene was, right from a movie. Maybe they'd have an innocuous conversation to counter the melodrama; maybe they'd try vainly to recover their old selves by racing to bed; maybe they would speak of him, laugh about the raffle tickets.

Janice, not Nora. He felt stifled, shot through with frustration. She said, "Would you believe I haven't been here since the service?"

His mind hadn't indulged such optimistic murmurs when he approached her in McCoy's. She didn't look familiar enough to start his gut's swirl of exquisite agony, yet once he recognized her, he couldn't blot out the feeling that the boy was with her, hiding behind the discounted shower stalls, waiting.

THE ELECTRICITY BLACKED OUT. WIND AND THUN-der coupled with darkness and lightning to give Nora enough courage—or fear, or pity—to nestle into his shoulder on the couch. Had he been standing, the smell of her hair, more oily than fragrant, would have buckled his knees. Water poured from the roof. Safety candles flickered on the coffee table. Sex crossed his mind, a breaking light of dangerous possibility, and the notion sent his heart racing; he hoped she couldn't feel it. He was unsure where to lay his hands, afraid to disturb the delicate air that was so mercifully tempered with her apprehension. Neither said anything, not even when she began to weep quietly into his chest. What, finally, could be said? Drifting to sleep, he imagined the candles igniting a gas leak; as the storm blew outside, he half wished it would turn the house to scrap.

No memory of retiring to Janice's room, but he found himself there—clothed, muscles stove-up, on top of the down comforter—waking, then tumbling back into sleep. A ragged dream: strolling with Nora through endless aisles of boats anchored in downtown streets. The vessels are on sale. A cluster of Karankawas, naked and wet and towering, with cane-pierced lips, browse as well. Nora worries the sale hasn't started yet; she puts her hand on his shoulder, and it stays there while they walk, as if she's blind. She says, "It's nice you're here." When he woke, she was not beside him, though she had been. He feared that whatever ease they'd enjoyed the night before, whatever comfort the storm had forged between them, would have vanished now, that the morning would have let the air out of Nora's lovely need.

She was watching the news, perched in front of a portable television. She wore a jaunty blouse and skirt of Janice's. Even these years later, he could tell that the clothes were borrowed.

She said, "They keep showing pictures of a drowned armadillo."

"Good morning to you, too."

"And film of the island. Turned-over boats, missing roofs. We slept through the worst of it."

His heart swelled: We.

The boarded windows dimmed the house, and the plywood's still being there pleased him. The room smelled of a velvety, sweetly nauseating perfume. She had opened the front door and the sun filtered in, a new light made brighter by the saturated lawns. Broken, waterlogged branches littered the street. A drenched basset hound trotted along the sidewalk, ambling past neighbors clearing detritus. From down the block, a woman's ecstatic voice: "Scooter! Scooter!" The dog stopped, perked up its ears, then loped homeward. Across the street, the architect inspected the taped X's on his tall windows; he was smaller than Sonny remembered, bald now. Wet leaves were plastered to the truck. On television the meteorologist advised viewers not to leave their homes; power lines were down and conditions were ripe for flash floods, lightning, funnel clouds and tornadoes. Defeat weighted his voice; Alicia, his lover, had left him. A map showing the storm's trajectory clicked on the screen. The eye had hit between Corpus and Kingsville; Sonny's prediction couldn't have been more wrong.

Nora poured coffee. He thought to say he drank only decaf, or to tell about the afternoon on the sixth green that had predicated the change, but he refrained. That day he'd enjoyed a fleeting cogent relief: Max wouldn't hear of this, wouldn't have to slog through an autopsy and funeral, wouldn't have to wonder about his father's pain or be mired in regret or recover. And he'd wondered when Nora, wherever she was, would receive the news. Now he accepted the coffee because he already felt weakened before her, felt scattered and drugged, and if she hadn't noticed his vulnerability yet, he didn't want to lay it bare.

"I've learned to make crepes." Then as if worried that she'd overstepped her boundary, she exhaled and slouched against the corner. "Or you probably need to get to work."

"We'll open at noon, if at all." More likely, he had phone messages asking him to come to work. He said, "Tomorrow everything will go on sale."

"Sonny . . ." She paused. Over her shoulder, he saw grackles in the yard, hunting beetles and earthworms. Two greenhouse windows were broken. Stalks of banana plants were snapped. She said, "Nothing."

He could've pressed, maybe she even wanted him to, but he let it go. Let it go, because whatever she would have said could have destroyed him, the words could have instantly unraveled the perfect lace of the night. The threat proved enough. Since finding her in McCoy's, he'd ignored how the corners of her eyes, tight and slightly, elegantly, upturned, resembled Max's. He'd ignored how after she left a room the air faintly carried the boy's powdery scent. Over the years, Sonny had naturally fitted himself to this role—grieving father, abandoned husband. Now such identities seemed self-aggrandizingly thin. And he realized the reason he'd skirted all the serious conversations had nothing to do with a fear that Nora would cave in again, but that he would. After she'd left, breaking down remained his one terror, and he'd clung to it like a lifeline.

She said, "This morning I remembered when they wanted to cut off our power, on Christmas Eve. You called and convinced them to leave it on, so we could light the tree for Max."

How long since he'd recalled that night, how long since he'd heard the name spoken aloud? She said it with such ease that Sonny felt cleaved from himself. And he knew she said it every day; like a prayer or confession, it absolved her.

"It was their mistake," he said. "We were square."

"That's what you always said. That was always sweet of you."

On television an anchorman interviewed a Port Aransas couple who'd lost everything. Missing person reports were coming in; bridges were washed out. Sonny didn't want to hear this and didn't want Nora to either. He said, "The newsman's a short fella, but you wouldn't know on television. He comes into McCoy's."

She cupped her hands around the coffee mug. A blush rose in her cheeks. Despite the clammy air that comes after storms, she looked cold and he expected her to shiver. Then, like that, she did. The room's brandy-tinged light and the air's fleeting, inexplicable scent of winter gave him the feeling of having crawled through a tunnel, of emerging to find Nora waiting for him. When she wasn't looking, he found his eyes could linger seconds longer than yesterday.

She said, "Janice told me you worked there. I was looking for you."

To his surprise, his answer didn't surprise him at all. He said, "I know."

THE FERRY ENGINE CHUGGED, TURNING OVER A frothy wake of the olive-hued water between Corpus and Port Aransas. They were due at a picnic for Coastal employees, the annual affair designed to build morale. In the truck bed was an ice chest with beer, mustard potato salad, peeled shrimp, cornbread. Nora and Sonny had bathing suits on under their clothes; Max wore his outright. He'd been grounded for a week and would remain so until Sunday, when he left for Camp Karankawa. But they had agreed he should be allowed to go to the picnic; they recalled how he'd loved last year's tug-of-war and sack races, how he'd caught a lightning bug in his mouth and the insect continued firing its harmless light on his tongue. Despite their best intentions to stay strict this week, their resolve had wavered. Nora had admitted to letting him watch cartoons after school, and Sonny confessed to telling Max his initiative would pay off in his adult life.

No raffle, no fund drive, no prize flight to AstroWorld. A neighbor had been boasting about his school's fund drive, so Max had invented his own campaign. He had made up the failing school budget, the depressed playground equipment, the impromptu district meeting that had so swiftly initiated the raffle. He'd already canvassed the neighborhood, come home, and situated himself in his room to denominate bills when Mrs. Dixon called Nora. She'd said, "I need him selling Avon!"

Sonny hoisted him onto the ferry's guardrail, kept his arm around Max's middle. He needed a haircut, and the wind blew back odd strands that tickled Sonny's neck, cheeks. Before the raffle, he was consumed with scouting, with securing his Karankawa badge, and before that he'd been a dramatist, drafting a play each afternoon, then casting his parents in after-supper productions. He'd written of mobsters and kings and aliens and pirates, and Sonny always felt that he'd not done the parts justice; nightly he'd seen his son be disappointed by his parents. But he'd also felt that he was in a luster, shining in the boy's reflected light. When he'd arrived home from the refinery and found Nora hanging up with Mrs. Dixon, she'd smiled and said, "Your son."

"Looky here," she said now, leaning over the port side. "Dolphins."

Porpoises, actually, four or five racing beside the boat, cameling their backs and jumping out of the water and diving in without a splash. They were dusk-colored—one almost black—their bellies glistening pink in the sun. Nora, he knew, was offering an olive branch, trying to rouse Max from sullenness. This was her way. Whereas Sonny waited for the smoke to clear, she lowered her head and barged in.

"Flippers," Max said. "Flippers!"

That is such a short float across the channel; usually most of the time is spent in traffic, waiting to get to the landing, but within a minute Max was growing antsy. Oh, youth. Hadn't

he just gotten a haircut? Sonny felt certain he had. He imagined the coming week, when he and Nora would have the
house to themselves, and he ignored how restricting Max had
been its own reward, keeping him at home, with them. This
seemed something he would admit one day, perhaps when
Max had a son of his own. *When will that be?* he wondered.
When will I have to wait to see you? As the ferry neared the
dock and the captain sounded the great horn, as the pod of
porpoises banked off to race the opposite boat and Sonny
helped his wife and son back into his small truck, their time
together threatened to pass within a breath.

I See Something
You Don't See

MINNIE MARSHALL NEEDED HER SON TO DRIVE her to the emergency room. Three in the morning, a Sunday in June; she had another migraine, a real monster that wasn't going to ease off without a Demerol injection. She hated to disturb Lee. In two weeks he would leave South Texas and return to St. Louis, return to the life she and the tumor in her lung had denied him for a year, and she wanted to let him rest. He'd already taken her three times in as many weeks, so to ask again also meant asking for his reticence or his lectures. She made herself wait. She tried sleeping and then reading, but when her vision began to blur and narrow, she crept into his dark room. She sat on his bed, touched his shoulder. When she whispered his name, her voice banged around in her head like a huge, frantic bird.

"I need a shot," she said. "It won't take long."

He lay on his stomach, offering no response. Her head throbbed, the chaotic pain replaced momentarily by a dull and familiar chiseling behind her eyes. She was fifty-three but had suffered migraines since childhood. After having Lee, she'd had a hysterectomy because a neurologist promised the procedure would snuff out the headaches. It didn't. During chemo and radiation, migraines had assailed her so frequently that the oncologist feared metastasis, but MRIs and CAT scans assured her otherwise. Just unlucky, the doctors had said.

Lee rolled onto his back. "They'll admit you."

"I just need a shot."

"They'll keep you overnight, maybe longer."

"Please," she said. The last thing she wanted was to cry, but her eyes pooled and her throat clenched. Then suddenly she feared she would vomit, too, and maybe pass out. She said, "Please, baby, I'm sick."

The ER was overcrowded. She almost asked Lee to go back to the car and take her to another hospital, but at least here the staff would recognize her. They would smile when she entered, lead her to the first available room and let her lie in darkness while Lee registered; the doctors would consult her file, ask if this one differed from the others, then send a nurse with an injection. The nurses called her "honey," asked about new Avon products, asked about Lee. If the nurse was pretty or especially gentle, Minnie would muster the energy to brag about Lee's teaching job in Missouri, his master's degree, everything he'd forfeited to come home and care for her; she would manage to leak that he was single, too. Tonight a heavy-jowled woman behind the registration desk noticed Minnie and made an exaggerated frown—*Again?* the frown asked—to which Minnie shrugged. Only one chair was available, so she sat while Lee waited to sign in. Beside her, a father cradled his sleeping son. There was a man with his hand wrapped in a wet towel; a hunched, wheezing woman who had fallen; a young woman having contractions. Other people were just waiting, their faces wrinkled with worry. She felt sorry for all of them.

An hour passed before a room opened, then another before a doctor arrived. He was new, with bloodshot eyes and a Pakistani or Indian name, Rama. He spoke quickly and without humor while his cold hands examined her too thoroughly. "A little fresh," she almost said, but refrained because neither Lee nor the doctor would have laughed. His manner was endearingly stiff; she'd always believed Lee would make a good doctor. When Rama left, she said, "I bet he's nervous, but excited."

She felt less generous when he ordered bloodwork and X-rays. Another half hour had slogged by. The migraine had its full claws on her now, and although the pain had put her on the verge of tears, news of the tests, which translated to more waiting, swept her over the edge. Lee tried negotiating with the nurse. He raised his voice, then pleaded and cited previous visits with successful dosages, but she wouldn't budge. It was only Rama's second night, she said, so he was overcautious. No one liked him—"Sheesh, we barely understand him," she said—but they had no choice. Wheeling the bed into the clattering, garishly lit hallway, the nurse whispered, "I'm sorry, honey."

When Minnie was finally returned to the room, Lee brought over a stool and stroked her hair. He rubbed her scalp, her closed eyes. His touch soothed her, as his father's had. There was no one time when she missed Richard the most—a misconception of those who'd never lost a spouse—but on nights when their son assumed a husband's role, Richard's absence seemed especially unjust, nothing more than a wanton punishment. She wasn't angry at him for dying—a misconception of therapists; she was angry that she'd survived. If she'd died instead, Lee would be sleeping in St. Louis, maybe in his own house with a wife and children, and not in an antiseptic-smelling emergency room, kneading her temples at the crack of dawn.

"You'll be glad when this ends," she said. Probably he fretted over what would happen when a migraine seized her after he'd left Corpus Christi. She fretted over it, too. "You'll make a good father."

"The apple from the tree, right?"

Yes, she thought, *yes.* She wanted to keep talking, but a leaden drowsiness draped over her like a blanket. She lay in the blue-black haze between sleep and waking, and waited for one or the other to claim her. She concentrated on staying still and not aggravating the pain; she forgot where she was, lost track of time. A gauzy memory of a motel pool, Richard belly flopping to amuse Lee. They are in Corpus, on Ocean Drive; no money for vacation that year. Richard bounces on the diving board, beating his chest like an ape. She could almost hear his voice, almost see his reddened stomach. Then, brightness:

a harsh, piercing light flooded the room and a nurse charged in with the syringe. The woman hurried, as if administering the Demerol on the sly, and said an ambulance had arrived and two more were following; a fire at the refineries. Minnie realized she'd heard the sirens, but had believed them a dream, the nightmare sirens that spirited Richard away every night. The hospital needed the room, the nurse said, so the dosage had been okayed without the test results.

"Great," Minnie said, stepping to the floor. "Perfect."

She smiled at Lee—the thrill that they'd scored a secret victory bloomed in her breast—then she lowered her pants and leaned over the bed. After the last year, he no longer needed to leave the room, and they all knew it. The injection pinched and burned, the Demerol felt thick as glue. Soon, though, her veins tingled pleasantly, her pain dissolving into velvet while the world's hard edges softened. She felt buoyant, as if floating in the motel pool, and while Lee signed release forms, the migraine faded, or her body did, and she became the turquoise water around her family. When Lee helped her to the car, the sun warmed her arms, and even with her eyes closed, she bathed in a golden, benevolent light.

HIS MOTHER'S ABSENCE WOKE HIM LIKE A BLOW to the chest. Lee was thirty-three but suddenly as frightened as a child. He checked each room, bracing himself to find her on the floor, fallen or hemorrhaging or catatonic from pills she'd swallowed to end the sorrow of living with cancer instead of a husband. Wednesday morning, she had no obligations. She'd slept most of yesterday, still sapped by the Demerol. Lately she spent mornings packing Avon orders, sorting mascara and powders on the backyard deck, but today it was abandoned. The house was empty.

He heard her trowel scraping on the bricks outside. His first impulse was to scold her for working in the sun when her skin could burn so easily. In truth, he wanted to punish her for worrying him, and he knew it. The year before, he'd walked away from his first teaching job and a volatile, makeshift relationship with the school's librarian to care for his mother as she underwent treatment; now he felt like a prisoner awaiting parole. Watching her through the window, he tried to take her gardening for what it was, evidence that she would live, evidence that in two weeks his life would resume.

"Someone was tired," she said as he stepped outside. Before he could reply, she added, "I'm wearing sunblock. SPF thirty."

A bolt of shame. The smell of coconut lotion and damp, fresh-turned soil recalled for him how often he'd found her here throughout his youth. He said, "Do you want breakfast?"

"I already ate. Yours is in the oven." Then, wiping her brow, she said, "I'm planting cannabis. If Avon peters out, I'll start dealing." Recently this was one of her favorite jokes, though he hadn't mustered a laugh even the first time she said it.

Her arms, blotched and bruised because her platelet count remained low, were glazed with sweat. Just ten o'clock, but the oily humidity had already swamped the morning. No wind blew, a ribbon of smoke spiraled up from an ashtray in the grass. She wore one of his old baseball caps, and a loose, plaid blouse with a denim collar. He said, "What's on your plate today?"

"I'll drop off more catalogs for the nurses. They're getting antsy."

Each week she left Avon books at the cancer center, and on weekends nurses and doctors' wives, patients and staff members phoned the house. They asked for her with as much reverence as Lee had once asked for the oncologist. Who would have pegged Minnie Marshall for such a sly hawker? Her customers ordered cosmetics and jewelry, toys and handbags, and hearing her pitch jasmine-scented creams pleased Lee in ways he couldn't remember feeling. The thought of her immersed in the work helped diffuse the guilt that haunted him for wanting to leave. He encouraged her, inquired about new promotions, and doted on the products she stockpiled on his behalf; he would never again want for roll-on deodorant. If he circled a cologne in a catalog, three bottles came with the shipment. Usually the aftershave arrived, too. "I thought maybe you'd missed it," she'd say.

Judging from the flower bed he guessed that she'd worked most of the morning. Probably she'd toiled for his sake, offering her efforts as further proof that she would be able to function without him. The garden was flourishing. He was admiring the marigolds and crape myrtle when the phone rang and she started pushing herself up from the ground. His heart flattened. Her balance hadn't yet recovered; she struggled slowly and awkwardly to stand, like a newborn colt. Her hair and energy had returned with her remission, but she still teetered after closing the refrigerator and had to fight to free herself from sofas with deep cushions. She was an old woman who wasn't old.

"Sit tight," he said. "I'll get it."

And although answering the phone seemed right, he was dismayed in the kitchen for not telling her to get out of the sun. Why, he wondered later, hadn't he? And why, when the man asked for Linda Marshall—not Minnie—did Lee say she wasn't home? Maybe he half recognized the accent, or maybe he couldn't face watching her stagger again.

"You are her son, correct?"

Lee said yes.

"I am Dr. Rama. I treated Mrs. Marshall for a migraine in the emergency room."

Lee said yes, okay.

"She must see her physician. Test results show . . ." Rama paused.

Lee felt himself breathing, heard the blood pulsing in his ears. He wanted to speak but was suddenly certain his voice would ruin something. He coiled and uncoiled the phone cord around his hand; he noticed the smells of bacon and toast that had lingered for hours, and his eyes locked on the refrigerator where banana magnets pinned down his mother's grocery list:

detergent, flour, butter, olive oil, chicken breasts, wine. His mouth tasted sour, like copper.

Rama said, "The tests are not good. There is aggressive metastasis to the brain."

Outside, his mother clapped soil from her gloves and picked an insect from a leaf. She inspected it, then lowered it to the yard. A cigarette dangled from her lips, the baseball cap swallowed her forehead and ears. She looked as he must have looked as an adolescent, bony and pale and vulnerable. He turned his back to her.

"I'll send results to her doctor," said Rama. "He will advise."

"Thank you," Lee said, though saying it struck him as strange.

He unwrapped his hand from the cord and hung up. He concentrated on the yellow magnets and his mother's grocery list—probably ingredients for Chicken Marsala, a dish she believed he liked more than he did—then he leaned his forehead against the refrigerator. He tried deciding what to do, for the first real decision of his life seemed upon him, but his mind blanked. He tried focusing himself with a question: *What should I do now?* Nothing came. The pressure to act bore down, as it would on a surgeon or soldier, a paramedic or murderer. Still, nothing. Until, finally, he steeled himself and aimed only to step outside and praise the work she had done this morning. If nothing else, he could grant her a last day in the sun.

———

THE DEMEROL HAD KNOCKED OUT THE MIGRAINE, AND Minnie had spent the last two days gardening and shopping and filling the goodie package she wanted to have waiting for Lee in Missouri. She'd neglected her Avon duties but looked forward to getting back on track. The work contented her as nothing had since losing Richard. Before the diagnosis, she'd worked as an accountant, a dull job that came easily, but such unfulfilling labor seemed fitting then. For six years, she'd thought enjoying herself would contradict how she missed her husband's body, his voice; joy felt like infidelity. But her remission seemed to have changed everything. She relished this new life, realizing that all along Richard would have been pleased by her happiness and that she'd been disappointing him. He deserved a widow who did more than fall to pieces when the sink clogged; Lee deserved a mother who managed more than withering in front of late-night infomercials; she herself deserved refuge from her grief. Sometimes when she visited with customers or cooked dinners for Lee, she thought, *So this is what I've missed.* She felt like someone back from war, awed by the changed country and how eagerly the crowds embraced her.

Undoubtedly, Lee worried that she would unravel without him. She had put him through so much, taking too many or too few pills when he wasn't home to supervise, not eating or sleeping, walking when she knew she would fall. Now she devoted herself to allaying his fears, to proving to him that her world would not crumble when he left. The goal was to send him back to St. Louis—she imagined it a bustling, sophisticated city in the shadow of the great Arch—and to get him back to his classroom and his half-finished dissertation on— what? Eighteenth-century labor codes? His imminent departure had ennobled her. She smiled and worked and pretended she was not terrified of being alone.

"You weren't very hungry," she said at the kitchen table. At most, he'd eaten half of his Chicken Marsala. "Do you want something else? I can order out."

"It's delicious. I'm just not feeling well tonight."

"Good news, then," she said. "I've got something to raise your spirits."

She sipped her iced tea, dabbed her napkin to her mouth. The parcel had arrived yesterday, but she'd kept it a surprise because he'd gone out last night. Withholding the news had been difficult but electrifying; all day she'd tried to imagine his reaction. She said, "I'm the district's top seller for this campaign."

"Well, gosh," he said, like a boy. He refilled her glass.

"Isn't that something? They sent me a plaque and a bonus check, and my name goes into a drawing for a Hawaiian vacation."

Lee looked shocked, uncomprehending. He said, "When did they send—"

"It's inspired me. I'll pass out more catalogs, more samples. Next year, we'll have an Avon empire!"

He cut another piece of chicken, then another, started eating again. "I'd say you've earned a rest. Why mess with the formula?"

"You're sweet," she said. "I feel just grand lately."

He finished his helpings, then spooned seconds onto his plate and polished those off. She knew he was proud of her, but still she could feel his dreariness and resolved to fix him a solid breakfast in the morning. She'd done as much when he was young, if he had a test or a soccer game. He'd preferred strawberry jam to syrup on his pancakes. Did he still?

She said, "The Hawaii trip isn't until next summer. I doubt I'll win, but who knows? Our luck seems to be turning."

"I don't think luck has much to do with it," he said, and dolloped mashed potatoes onto his plate.

She felt herself glowing. *So this is what I've missed.*

THE TEST RESULTS HADN'T REACHED THE ONCOLO-gist by Thursday. When Lee explained the situation to Dr. Wood, she reacted with such skepticism that he briefly let himself think he'd misunderstood everything. He'd been waiting for the dementia to expose itself, but his mother split ferns and distributed catalogs and hung the Star Seller plaque over the television. Almost hourly he decided to tell her the bad news, then quickly reversed his decision.

On Friday afternoon, he called Dr. Wood again and felt ambushed, then contritely validated, when she said the results did indeed indicate a rapid spread to his mother's brain. Her tone was solemn and regretful, and stricken, as if by the cancer's audacity. She ordered more tests for the coming week, then outlined further treatments. Lee knew his mother would refuse them—"When pigs fly," she'd said when Dr. Wood previously suggested prophylactic radiation—so he asked the doctor, who suddenly seemed in his debt, what would happen without treatment. Her answer came quickly. His mother might live a few months, perhaps six or eight, though her motor skills and her ability to care for herself would begin to shut down. Her sight and hearing would diminish, muscles would atrophy. She would become incontinent, bedridden. She would forget the most fundamental information: her name and his, how to chew, swallow, and speak.

Lee asked, "Will she know what's happening?"

"I'm not sure I follow," Wood said.

"If no one explains it."

"Oh," she said, then paused. "Lee, she's a trouper. More radiation could slow, or possibly stop, the metastasis."

He imagined his mother turning to him upon receiving the news, her eyes clouded with disbelieving panic. Or would she hide behind a veil of smug morbidity? No matter, however she heard the diagnosis, it would rip the rug out from under her. She was not one for surprises. She was not a trouper.

Wood's voice softened. "And you don't have to tell her, Lee. But as her physician, I'm obligated to when I see her."

He caught himself wrapping the phone cord around his hand again. How peculiar that his thoughts went to the librarian in St. Louis; a week before he'd learned of his mother's

———

tumor, the woman had come into his classroom and accused him of being unable to accept kindness.

On the phone, he cleared his throat and asked the doctor, "What if you don't see her?"

MINNIE DIDN'T UNDERSTAND WHY THE INSURANCE company needed another MRI, or why Lee had mentioned the appointment only the night before. She had started to argue, then relented. Lee had been distracted and addled lately, she thought, given to an absentmindedness that reminded her of his first days of grade school. She had tried to bolster him then—the good breakfasts, afternoon Popsicles, trips to the toy store his father didn't know about—as this past year he had tried to rally her. In their last week together, she welcomed her role back again.

They sat in the waiting room of the radiology lab—not at the cancer center but in a hospital across town—and she drank the syrupy, cherry-flavored liquid they gave her before MRIs. "There's a new cologne this month," she said. "It's called Rodeo."

"I'll take three," he said. He was flipping through a magazine. He hadn't shaved; his eyes looked bleary.

"The nurse has taken a shine to you," she said. "Want me to fake a seizure?"

She'd expected him to laugh or glance at the blonde behind the registration desk, but he said, "She'd call the doctor."

"Maybe the doctor's cute, too."

The nurse checked her makeup in a compact mirror. Minnie wished she'd brought catalogs to leave on the orange chairs.

"Lee," she said quietly, "is something on your mind, baby?"

"I'm sorry?"

"Are you nervous about going back?"

He tipped his head to his shoulder, his eyes returning to an article. He said, "There's just a lot to do before school starts."

"You put so much pressure on yourself. Daddy did, too."

She finished another cup of the syrup, thinking vaguely of Richard, of his hands, how Lee's fingers resembled his. She recalled Richard carving a turkey before they were married, maybe their first holiday together, when she already loved him so much she could hardly breathe.

"I was thinking I'd come up for Thanksgiving," she said. The words surprised her as much as her voice. Such an idea had never occurred to her before, but now it was enticing; now it was a trip she'd always wanted to take. "I'd love to see the fall leaves. I can cook for you."

"Maybe I'll come down here. The weather will be nicer."

"No," she said. "I'd like to visit you. I intend to start traveling more."

In the MRI machine, it was not lassitude that descended but an unexpected zinginess. She felt like a child on a playground, shooting through a tube slide. The air smelled steely. The cylinder's ceiling hung an inch above her; she touched her nose to it, just for a goof. Cold. The machine whirred and thumped and clanked, then went silent for a spell before the racket resumed. During one of the silences she said, "Kiss a fish" and made herself laugh. How long since she'd heard that? During the years when Lee had resented having his picture taken, Richard would say it to make him smile. "Kiss a fish," she said again, louder, then laughed again. How strange to hear her cackle reverberate, ever so slightly echo; she would mention that to Lee later. She tried to imagine him starting a conversation with the blond nurse. He'd blink twice before each sentence, look at his hands while he spoke; if things went well or very badly, he'd find something to fidget with. She knew, though, that he was sitting in the same orange chair, poring over a wrinkled magazine.

Then, instantly, time started dragging. Sweat on her forehead, under her arms. Her spine ached and her nose itched; she felt a sneeze coming, but couldn't move enough to let it go; she flexed her toes, heard them pop like twigs. In high school she'd learned it wasn't the joints themselves, but bubbles of sinovial fluid bursting between bones; that was the year she and her girlfriends sprawled on the beach, sharing cigarettes and mixing iodine with baby oil for darker tans. What a thing to recall. The machine cycled again, the noises grinding more harshly, as if unbuffered. A grating thrum seemed centered over her chest; the cylinder seemed to tighten, the ceiling seemed to lower. An acute terror: What if the exam revealed something unexpected and she detained Lee another five months? Assuming he'd stay; maybe such news would be the last straw. Then, strangely, as if allowing the thought to form nullified its possibility, the terror dispersed. She sighed to hear herself sigh. Now she only wanted lunch and a cigarette, to be freed from the cylinder, to become the child dropped from the slide onto the sand. Hawaii. Ukulele music and umbrellas in tangerine-colored drinks. How much darker would the nights be on the island, how much brighter the stars? Had Richard ever been? She had a vague memory of him liking the Pearl Harbor museum. She imagined forcing herself to mingle, telling tourists about Richard and Lee, about living in Corpus and about her remission, then she would hear about their lives until the time came to ask if they'd like some catalogs. She smiled at the idea of appearing in random snapshots; years later, the photos would be rediscovered and the viewer would eventually find her in a slippery, pleasant recollection: the Avon lady.

LEE FIXED HIS EYES ON THE ARTICLE WHILE A WAVE of shock rose in his chest. His muscles tensed. Nothing had been settled with Dr. Wood, but she'd convinced him that regardless of treatment, an MRI was necessary to assess the extent of the metastasis. She'd scheduled the tests at this lab because it was more expeditious than her own; he'd brought his mother under the pretense of an insurance company request. But she seemed suspicious. Her questions were snares, and he was misremembering what he had and hadn't told her. And now this: "Is something on your mind, baby?" His thoughts scrambled to find the letter he'd left on a table, the phone message he'd not erased, a doctor's call he'd not been home to intercept. *This is where you'll tell her,* he thought.

This is where she'll find out, in a waiting room with old magazines and orange-cushioned chairs.

MEXICAN FOOD AFTER THE MRI. HER IDEA. DURing chemo, she'd craved enchiladas and assured Lee and herself that if she ate slowly and responsibly, she wouldn't get sick. Or she had assured Lee, but told herself the retching wouldn't strike until later, an acceptable consequence for tasting something more than rice cakes and chalky protein drinks. But that afternoon she had vomited into her plate after only a few bites, and today the smell of *pico de gallo* shamed her.

"My file was marked 'Urgent,'" she said after the waiter left the check. "I saw it on the way out."

"Go figure," Lee said. "They probably consider all insurance work urgent."

He took a long drink of water. Around the restaurant, red, white, and green streamers trimmed the windows. Years before, on road trips and in pediatricians' waiting rooms, they'd had a game. She'd say, *Riddle Miraddle Marie, I see something you don't see, and the color is black,* or maybe *yellow* or *purple,* and he'd try to name whatever she'd spied.

He said, "They probably get paid more quickly if it's marked urgent. Company policy."

"I wasn't supposed to get tested for another six months. Maybe something's wrong."

He sighed, lidded his eyes. "Let's give this a rest, okay?"

"I don't see why they need more exams. I get scared, honey."

"You're looking for something to scare you."

She lit a cigarette, shook out the match. He was right.

He reviewed the bill and motioned for the waiter. He said, "We'll be fine."

THE DILEMMA CONSUMED HIM, AND THE MORE HE considered it, the more withholding the news seemed appropriate, merciful. Whatever time remained would not be marred by a clock ticking in her head; it would tick in his alone. Contriving reasons for not returning to work would be easy enough—he'd already canceled his flight and contacted the school's principal. Then he could concentrate on making her last months comfortable. That, he thought, was what his father would do. He could start cooking her meals again, rent movies, read to her. They could play cards and work puzzles, the pieces growing larger and thicker as her faculties failed. He could drive her into the Hill Country, to the beach. He could take her to Hawaii.

What he could not do was ignore a passing, but potent realization: He knew that every word of his staying to care for his mother, and word of her dying, would eventually find Moira Jarrett, his old friend Russell's sister and maybe the only woman he'd ever loved. For the last year he'd stayed immune to the encroaching, regrettable thrill that came with imagining how Moira would react to all he'd endured, but now he would succumb to it. And now became clear the twofold feeling of escape he'd enjoyed when he thought he was leaving: His mother was safe from cancer and he was safe from memories of Moira. In the few times he'd seen Russ since returning to Corpus, he'd avoided talk of his sister, and he'd taken pride in how little he knew of her life. Now that he saw the hopelessness of his guardedness, he wondered why he'd ever struggled to deny himself. Because there seemed a certain dignity in not admitting how vividly the city recalled her for him? Because when he and Moira were dating, his mother had called her trashy and warned him of women who trap men with pregnancies? Moira had never known about this, and despite her leaving him years before, Lee knew she wouldn't miss his mother's funeral; that he understood this, that the understanding awoke a fluttering optimism in him, left him nettled and nauseous. Regardless of terms like *misplaced guilt* and *coping mechanisms* that he'd read in Dr. Wood's caregiver's manual, he could no longer trust his motives, either toward himself or toward his mother.

"Oh," she said when he mentioned postponing his flight. She sounded taken aback, as if she'd planned on renting out his room. They were in the den, watching television; a stratum of cigarette smoke hung over their heads. He said he'd overestimated his prep time and could stay another two weeks, at least. "Well, super," she said at a commercial. "I'll go to the store tomorrow. We'll need more food."

That night it clicked for the first time that denying her this choice could be unforgivable, tantamount to holding a pillow over her face as she slept. Perhaps the doctor would be right, perhaps her decision would surprise him. Maybe the remission had so restored her spirit that more radiation would seem easy and she'd be baffled by his distress. He lay in bed, hearing her laugh, then cough, through the wall. He imagined barging into the den and delivering the news in a single breath. Then it would be over. She would be confused and shocked, but soon her newfound optimism would kick in. She would draw him near, massage his temples with fingers that smelled of lilacs and nicotine. She would say, "There, there. It's okay now."

He started watching her with pity—lamenting her wax-yellow skin, her miserable, unflinching optimism—and he thought telling her would make her less pitiful. But it also seemed selfish—a cop-out to ease his own burden, not hers. Or perhaps he lacked such courage and simply cowered from bearing the worst news. For two weeks he'd viewed himself as trying to save her, like a trainer poised to throw in the towel for his outmatched boxer; now he realized that the longer he remained alone with the information, the longer he himself was saved.

They were working in the garden when she said, "We should still arrange my funeral. Even if I live another fifty years, it's a good idea."

"Maybe we can arrange mine, too. Buy one, get one free."

"I'm serious, Lee. I'm thinking pragmatically."

Even in the incandescent sun, he felt chilled. Color flushed or left his cheeks—he couldn't tell which. She scattered hibiscus seeds in the soil, and he wondered if the blooms would eventually make him weep. He wondered how long his weeping would last. Finally he said, "You're right."

"And I have a living will. You have power of attorney, so we'll be set."

He kept quiet for fear of betraying himself. He felt it coming, the gravity of inevitability, but didn't want to surrender thoughtlessly. He intended to rehearse the words and prepare responses, to anticipate her reactions and stand ready to fight and console her.

"I ordered your new cologne. Rodeo."

He smoothed the soil. His mind strove to find a joke, something about lassos or cowgirls or horses, but nothing came.

"You seem preoccupied," she said.

"Yes," he said. "Or no. Yes and no."

She removed her gloves, took a sip of water. Her tumbler perspired. Flecks of soil clung to her neck. He wanted to brush them away but feared his touch would tear her skin. She said, "Let's go inside."

"No, I'd like to stay here. Sitting here suits me." His tone was too pensive; he felt the stress creasing his brow; he felt his mother's eyes lingering.

She took another drink. She appeared neither anxious nor worried but resigned to whatever he would say, as she must have been when he was young, when she could glue whatever he'd broken. She lit a cigarette, blew the smoke over her shoulder, away from him. And, briefly, he felt absolutely and desperately calm, himself resigned to whatever the future held. His calm was not born of hope—and perhaps, he feared, neither was hers—but of hope's absence. He had never expected her to live. Even when news of remission enveloped and intoxicated them like the smell of a new, beautiful home, and even when they confirmed and celebrated their luck with plans for the coming years, he had never trusted her recovery. Since her initial diagnosis, he'd known but never admitted that she wouldn't survive; he'd started mourning her on the afternoon she called him home. Now his last obligation was to wait.

"So what is it?" she asked.

"School," he said. "The district's laying off teachers. It might be a year before I can go back."

LATELY SHE'D STARTED WONDERING WHAT KIND of mother she'd been, too lax or strict, too clingy or absent; she wondered how, when the time came, Lee would remember her. When he was young, she had forbidden movies his friends were allowed to watch, and had sometimes done his homework when he was ill. She'd insisted he play only touch football but let him wear a Mohawk. She'd given him condoms too early, and called him too often at college. She had fallen apart when his father died, and she had never recovered. She had convinced him she would live when he moved to St. Louis, then she had dragged him home again.

Originally, she had considered not telling him of the disease. He'd been in Missouri for two years, happy and thriving, and she didn't want to interfere. And she was more scared of the treatments than of dying. She knew the misery of chemo, knew radiation guaranteed nothing. After her doctor said "cancer," she'd tried writing a letter for Lee to find afterward, but the words sounded feeble, clumsy. How to tell your son you've decided not to go on? Then suddenly she found herself on the phone with him, spilling the diagnosis and sobbing because she was afraid of everything. She had endured the treatment to keep him beside her, but recovering had never been more than a distant, cursory consideration, like a roadside attraction she might stop to see if time allowed. She had never wanted to live, had only wanted not to die alone.

Tonight she waited until he'd eaten and relaxed before saying anything. They watched television in the den, then when the timing felt right, she said, "No more treatment."

He looked caught, trapped, astonished. Poor thing.

She exhaled smoke, stabbed out her cigarette. "I delivered Dr. Wood's Avon a few days ago."

The consternation on Lee's face made her feel as if she'd told him of some metastasis in his own body. Her heart lurched; she wanted nothing more than to gather him in her arms and apologize, but she didn't move. She saw him gauging what would be best to say, what would be worst. Richard had done this, deliberated each word or thought before granting it voice. It was considerate and nerve-racking. She lit another cigarette, forced herself to feel the cold-hot cloud in her lungs. She stopped expecting him to deny the implications of what she'd said. Rather, she tried to stop. For days she'd struggled to purge such a prospect from her mind, and though she'd mostly succeeded, times came when she indulged herself, like sneaking a bite of cookie dough. Grandchildren, the trip to Hawaii, seeing Lee's life unfold. Now she needed to stay composed and discard everything except his silence that confirmed her dying.

"I'm not angry," she said.

He nodded. Maybe he said that he'd planned on telling her, that he'd decided he must and was only awaiting the right time, but she heard very little. Her pulse raced. Her skull pounded. Undoubtedly this would spawn a migraine. She told herself to stay calm, to take deep breaths, to bear up. Then, at the oddest moment, a memory: Lee, in third grade, doing magic at a talent show. She had sewn his costume, fashioned a top hat from posterboard, and Richard had paged through a book of beginner illusions with him. He hadn't won the contest—Who had? The pigtailed soprano? The brothers staging the detective play?—so afterward she and Richard treated him to ice cream. Vividly, she recalled thinking such a night was all she'd ever wanted, thinking for half an hour that she'd known precisely what life was for; it was for this.

In the den, Lee said, "There *is* treatment. The doctor—"

"No more."

She'd anticipated him getting righteous and angry and lobbying for radiation. Her mind stayed poised to grapple with him, to spar until he agreed to let the disease run its course. But he didn't argue. His silence disoriented her. Suddenly time needed filling, and in those still, hushed moments she realized it: They would never fight again. Starting now, their lives would fray and splinter and speed away from each other. All of their future interactions would be strained pleasantries, empty and courteous conversations that meant nothing except I'm sorry or good-bye.

"Thank you," she said.

"For what?"

"For not gunning for treatment. I appreciate it."

Another slow, defeated nod as he turned to peer out the sliding glass doors to the deck. Already she felt herself acclimating to this last experience of her life, succumbing, like someone who after days of treading water finally goes under without surprise or regret. Again she thought of Lee's talent show, pictured him alone on stage making her scarves disappear, then for the grand finale, bringing them back.

After another cigarette, she said, "I've got more news."

"Okay," he said, guardedly.

"I won the Hawaii trip."

What else could he have said: "I'm sorry."

AFTER HIS MOTHER DRIFTED TO SLEEP, LEE WENT through the house turning off lights. He felt as if he'd duped her. Perhaps a shred of that feeling stemmed from not telling her, but most of the guilt seethed in a less identifiable place. He realized he'd had more hope than he'd admitted; he realized this because now it was gone.

When he returned to the den, she was still asleep in the recliner. The glow of the television illuminated the room. Pictures of himself lined the walls, photos that seemed disconnected from him now, boys he'd never known. Hanging slightly askew among them was the Avon plaque. He almost reached to straighten it, but just then he was loath to disturb anything she'd touched; those chores would come. He watched her sleep, and her every breath seemed a sheaf of life itself. He wondered if would feel anything when she passed, some alarm or rupture or seizing up in his body. *Your mother has died,* he thought—even allowed the words to take shape in his mouth, tasting how they would hollow and shamefully exhilarate him. He thought of Moira Jarrett, imagined how over the next months he would lose the wherewithal to rebuke himself and would surrender to the whim of her memory without apology. He imagined wrapping the Avon plaque in a towel, packing it with the pictures. What else would he keep, what would get sold? Despite himself, he would start assessing her effects this way, categorizing them in terms of Sell, Donate, Trash. At breakfast tomorrow he would appraise the table and chairs, the dishes and cutlery, her robe, slippers and rings. And what would he find that he'd not known about? Love letters from his father, a diary? A childhood drawing he'd made for her, newspaper clippings about his graduations and meager achievements? Or would other, more innocuous things crush him? Half-finished crossword puzzles or a stash of chocolate, a postcard he'd sent her or a cut-out recipe. He began wondering what she had kept from him because now it seemed he'd kept everything from her.

MINNIE HADN'T SEEN OR SPOKEN TO DR. WOOD. Still, she knew the news as surely as if she'd sat in the doctor's office and studied the test results herself. For days she'd bided her time, considered how to approach Lee. She thought the strategy she had finally chosen would prove less taxing, less painful for both of them. Get it over with, pull the bandage off quick.

She pieced together how he had come to know of the metastasis, but had she not suspected it already, she would not have recognized its clues. She had sensed the presence in her body just as a young mother can sense her child long before learning she's pregnant. She regretted Lee's dwelling on the news alone, and anger welled inside her—maybe where hope had been—toward herself and toward the new doctor who must have disclosed the information. She considered calling his superior, thought of suing the hospital, a lawsuit that would outlive her but one that might yield good money for Lee. Swiftly, though, the idea lost air. She realized Rama might make a fine doctor, one who only wanted his patients to get the care they needed. In time she would forgive herself, too, or at least forget what she'd ever thought she'd done wrong.

And she reaccustomed herself to the idea of dying. Her remission had lasted almost five months, and she regarded the time as a vacation, as a brief though pleasurable stint on an island. But now she found herself home again, returned to a familiar routine. Fear returned too, of course, and moments came when it hammered her, struck so hard that she felt nothing else and had to sit to save herself from falling. But fear had come with the remission as well—who would understand this?—the terror of relapse, and a different terror, of living another twenty years, another thirty. Lee stayed on. She unpacked the box she'd intended to have waiting in Missouri; she gave him the contents one by one, when she remembered.

If she knew he was away, picking up a prescription or grabbing dinner when neither of them felt like cooking, she let herself cry. She wept for all she had lost, all she had taken and would take from her son, and for all she would lose before, at last, she herself was relieved.

Before drifting off on the night she had confronted Lee, Minnie said, "I'll keep working as long as I can. The money helps."

He nodded, though probably he suspected she would start staying home more, as she did.

"Who knows," she said, "maybe we'll make it to Hawaii after all. Or somewhere else. I'd like to get out of Texas for a while."

"Sure. Anywhere you want."

"That's our next project, a much-needed vacation. We'll keep our chins up. This doesn't have to mean the end of the world."

"No," he said. "It doesn't have to mean that at all."

She could have said more, but a comfortable silence settled over them and Minnie closed her eyes. There would be time to talk tomorrow and the next day and the next. For the moment, she liked the quiet and felt neither scared nor in pain; she was just tired, and only wanted Lee to sit with her as she went to sleep. Really, as with us all, that was all she'd ever wanted, someone to watch over her, someone who would lie and tell her not to be afraid, someone who would always, always say, Don't worry, I'm here.

In the Tall Grass

MY FATHER IS REMOVING HIS RINGS. WE ARE outside of Corpus Christi, Texas, on a ranch owned by a man named Edwin Butler. A busted gate hangs open behind us, and the odor of mud and horses seeps into the cab of our small truck. This is 1979, a year when my mother's spirits remained low and I was fourteen and my father wore three rings. He has not been arrested yet, and while that comes soon enough, he is already gone from me, as distant as the ice-blue snow of my dreams.

George Kelley, my father, had slender hands; on another man, his trimmed nails and long fingers might have been good for playing the piano. He worked at the Naval Air Station, building ship engines, and although most men in his shop were enlisted, his was a civilian job that he'd lucked into after serving in the Coast Guard down in Mississippi, where he was born. My father left for work early, when our floors were cold and the house and morning were without light. Often the sounds of his getting up woke me too, though I soon slipped back to sleep, after hearing him shave and dress and say "I love you" to my mother.

They'd met in 1964. My mother was waitressing at the Esquire Club, where my father enjoyed eating dinner and playing cards. Her name was Price then, Marie Price, because she was waiting for a man in Boston to sign annulment papers—his name was also George. My father was twenty-five, himself divorced from a woman in Mississippi; my mother was nineteen. Within a month she'd moved into his apartment, and a year later a judge married them and they honeymooned in Mexico. A black-and-white photo someone had taken of her hung on their bedroom wall, my mother wading in the Gulf, looking young and delicate and happy.

But my mother also suffered from depression and often refused to leave her room for days at a time. She took pills to raise her mood, but sometimes those failed and my father called her boss and she stayed in bed. Occasionally, my parents spoke of an operation, a hysterectomy, which a doctor had suggested, but they distrusted that procedure and talked of it only, I thought, to reassure themselves that they agreed about not having it. During these days my mother lived on Cokes and cigarettes and chocolate, and she liked me to sit beside her and talk. The lights in her room remained off, and always before I entered, I knocked to warn her, to allow her time to compose herself or cover her head with the pillow.

We discussed programs she'd watched on television. Or my days at school. Or she examined me in the dim light and noted how I had my father's posture but her skin and eyes, attributes that girls would eventually find beautiful. Sometimes I answered questions she'd thought up earlier in the day. How did I picture myself in ten years? Twenty? Had I kissed girls? Had I drunk alcohol or smoked cigarettes? Usually I spoke honestly, but sometimes I embellished or contrived answers to make her smile or, with luck, laugh.

In the spring of 1979 my father was a shift supervisor, and wore ties and slacks instead of coveralls. My mother worked at the high school I would attend that fall; she was the principal's secretary. The previous year someone from my father's shop had given us two horses because he needed space on his property and didn't want to hassle with selling them. My father had handled horses before and knew my mother had enjoyed riding lessons as a girl, so he arranged two stalls at Edwin Butler's ranch and drove four hours south to Mexico for cheap blankets and saddles.

My mother's horse was named Lady, a black thoroughbred, fourteen hands high, and too big for her to ride with any control. On her back, my mother looked like a child. Mine was a brown-and-white gelding that I named Colonel because of a white star on his shoulder. He'd won trophies for running barrels in the past and that excited me because I longed for a trophy then and lacked any skills to earn one.

Because my father arrived at the naval base early, most afternoons he left in time to pick me up at school and drive to the stables. We usually arrived earlier than the other owners, and sometimes in those hours before my mother met us there or before Edwin Butler unlocked the steel gate to give trucks access to the stable area, my father saddled Lady and we rode together. Horses responded to my father, obeyed his commands in ways they didn't for other men. Although his belly rolled over his belt, my father could swing himself onto a horse in a single swift, graceful motion. He rode fast and hard. When he dug his heels into Lady's sides and hollered for her to come on, she exploded into a run so loud and strong and gorgeous that it made you gasp. Leaning close to her mane, he held the reins with one hand and clapped her backside with the other; they were nothing but run. Colonel struggled to follow, but Lady's legs powered ahead until we fell back and could only listen to them ride.

It was on a day when I hoped we might ride together that trouble came about. We had not ridden much that week; a storm in the Gulf had soaked Butler's corral. And my mother's spirits had been low—her mood usually suffered in bad weather. Men from my father's shop were being laid off, friends of his who had worked there longer than he had, and he'd been taking overtime, having me catch the bus from school. So it surprised me to see him that afternoon, parked outside in his little Toyota truck. But I liked finding him there, and remember thinking he looked pleased.

"Was today a good day?" he asked as I ducked into the cab. He wore a lavender tie and gray slacks and musky cologne. His boots were shined, though I don't know if I noticed that in the truck or later. His lunch box sat on the floorboard, a thermos rattling as the engine idled. My father smiled. He was growing a beard. "Are you smarter than you were yesterday?"

"Maybe," I said. "It was okay."

"And math? How was that old bear?"

Math had given me trouble that year, and every evening after returning from the stables, my father worked equations with me, hoping I wouldn't have to repeat the course in the fall. "Better," I said. "We review on Fridays."

"Say, Benny, did I ever tell you what my favorite math problem was when I was in grade school?" We were waiting to exit the parking lot and he was watching traffic, staring away from me. "Seven times seven," he said, accelerating onto the street. "I remembered that today. It's a strange thing to recall, I guess. Maybe I liked the symmetry of it."

And although he was talking in an unusual way, using too many words, I understood him. My father enjoyed numbers because they were absolute, and linked with money and credit, words that in our family carried the weight of religion.

We turned into South Shore Estates, a neighborhood of two- and three-story homes, all surrounded by a brick wall. It was a route we had not taken before. Sailboats occupied many of the driveways, and a golf course fanned out behind the houses. I could smell the ocean.

"Do you wish you lived in a house like these?" he asked.

I did wish that, and wished it often, but I said, "No," and when my father made no response, I added, "Not at all." We lived in a two-bedroom wood-frame house on the corner of Longcommon Road, across from a mechanic's garage.

"Your mother used to live this way." He ran his fingers through his hair, which was dark and combed straight back. "I'm sure she misses it, too."

My father eased off the gas and slowed enough that I thought he was listening for something in the engine. He lowered his window and craned his neck outside. All of the girls I liked from school lived in South Shore, and although I felt guilty for it, I hoped they wouldn't see me with my father in their neighborhood. He steered with one hand and the truck veered to the wrong side of the street.

Then he raised his window and gave the engine some gas. "There's a small problem at the stables." My father opened his hands and stretched his fingers so only his palms rested on the steering wheel, then he tightened his grip. "Not with the horses, don't worry on that. It's a misunderstanding with our man Butler." He pushed the clutch and went to shift gears, but the transmission was already in fourth, so he had nowhere to go and let it alone. "He called your mother today, claimed we missed this month's rent. She says she paid it, but we'll hear him out. There's time for that."

We curved onto Yorktown Road, which would take us to Butler's ranch, and began heading south. My father passed cars traveling slower than us. An unfinished house, just a skeleton of studs on a foundation, stood in a hay field to our left, a snarl of mesquite branches stacked by the road.

"Do you know," my father said suddenly, "what I've seen your mother doing these last few nights?"

"No," I said. "What?"

"Feeding ants." He chuckled and shifted his eyes to me, shaking his head. "They're rebuilding their mound beside the house, but the rain keeps catching them. She slips out there and sprinkles popcorn over them."

I remembered seeing the anthill and could picture my mother crouching beside it. "Was she sad?"

"No." He straightened himself on the seat. "No, she smiles and is content to feed those ants. It's a relief to her, I guess."

A sign marking the city limits stood to our left and my father snapped his fingers and pointed at it. "We're free men." His voice came out flat, though it sounded like a joke to me.

The road narrowed to two lanes and ran alongside shallow ditches, where weeds extended from brackish water. My father loosened his tie, removed it, and folded it on the seat between us. "We should buckle our seat belts," he said, so we did that. We rode beside a cornfield and I watched the rows of soil tick by, trying to focus on the point where they converged at the horizon. My father rolled down his window again and extended his arm outside, the air slicing around it, creating the illusion of wind.

"A person can care too much." He raised his voice. "Does that make sense to you right now?"

"Yes," I said. "It does."

"You're smarter than me," he said, then laughed. I faced him and laughed, too, because he did. He squeezed my shoulder. And I thought of my father as a boy, something I could do easily then. It was my habit to compare his youth to my own and question the ways our lives already differed. The images lacked any colors except black and white, and it seemed a time when things moved faster, not slower, as you might guess, but like an old movie where the film speeds from frame to frame without sound or pause.

LIKE MOST MEN, EDWIN BUTLER STOOD TALLER than my father but limped from a knee operation that kept him from working. He collected checks from the government, and when they arrived, he went to bet on the dogs in Annaville. His wife was a long-haired woman named Deidra who bred Dalmatians for a living, but I'd seen other women step out of Edwin Butler's house trailer. A plywood sign stood in their little yard—a cowboy riding a whale under the words SEAHORSE RANCH. The property was only ten miles from the ocean, maybe less than that, but out there you couldn't smell the water or know that you were close to it at all.

"No one's here yet," my father said.

In a pen beside Butler's trailer, two Dalmatians rose and watched through their fence as my father steered into the parking area. Horses and a few cows grazed in the pasture, their legs and bellies caked with mud, and Lady stood in her stall, flipping her tail at the gnats and mosquitoes that always appeared after rain.

Instead of parking close to our stalls, my father cut the tires toward the house trailer and angled the truck back toward the street. He braked. I asked what was wrong, but he said nothing and I picked up the faint murmur of voices on the radio, which I hadn't realized was playing. We rolled forward, then stopped and my father shifted gears, unbuckled his seat belt, and twisted to look through the back window. And suddenly he punched the gas. The truck gunned backward—it felt as though we were in a free fall—and we slammed into Edwin Butler's steel gate. My safety belt locked across my chest; the gate rattled. A low, thin pitch rang in the air. I saw, or felt, horses spook in their stalls, retreat to opposite corners with their ears pinned back. The Dalmatians froze, their heads cocked toward the sky. And although I was staring at my father, he never looked at me but just shifted gears and accelerated forward, then stopped and reversed into the gate again, busting the lock and swinging it open.

Edwin Butler parted the curtains in his window and squinted at us, then he nodded and the curtains fell together. I was holding on to the seat, the muscles in my arms and ankles flexing. The trailer door opened after a moment, a long moment in which everything stood very still and the only noise was a disc jockey's laughter on the radio. When Butler stepped outside, my father cut the ignition. "Here it is," he said.

In a pink T-shirt, jeans and ostrich-hide boots, Butler puckered his face as though it had been dark inside the trailer. A truck passing on Yorktown honked and he saluted the driver, smiling. "That's right," my father said. "Keep it up." He shifted his weight and removed his wallet, stashed it under the seat. "Don't let me forget that." I said okay but couldn't tell if he heard my answer. His eyes stayed on Butler, who'd squatted to wipe mud from his boots. And as we sat there, waiting and not speaking, my father pulled off his rings.

He closed his fist around them, not for more than a second, but long enough for me to know he meant to hold the rings that way; I thought he might be talking himself into something, or out of something, maybe out of a decision he'd already made. Then he reached over and pressed them into my hand. His palms and fingers felt warm, as did the rings. "Keep these in your pocket," he said. "Your old man might go to jail tonight."

I answered my father by saying, "Yes, sir," something I'd never said before. I felt myself breathing.

"Now go say hello to those horses," he said. "They'll want to see you today."

Butler was closer to the truck now, skirting a puddle as my father stepped outside. I looked at him then, turning and starting toward Butler, and he appeared normal. Nothing crazy burned in his eyes and he wasn't rushing, but everything else seemed unfamiliar, part of another boy's life.

"I thought I'd see you pretty soon," Butler said. "I tell you what." Then he laughed a high laugh. I opened my door and eased it closed after stepping out. Butler looked at me, as if my presence might explain something to him, but when it didn't, he turned back to my father. The Dalmatians chased each other, their black-and-white tails wagging; horses whinnied.

If Butler expected anything, it was for my father to push or curse him or, at worst, to swing at him with his right fist, with a hook or a straight punch from the chest. Probably my father realized this. Earlier in his life, he'd fought a lot—I'd heard that—so what my father did to Butler shouldn't have shocked me. But I was fourteen, and when it happened, my stomach clenched and I covered my face.

He kicked him in his bad leg, just lunged forward and brought his heel and all of his weight down onto Butler's kneecap. The joint popped, made a *thwack* sound, and buckled. I felt the impact in my chest, on my skin, and, without meaning to, I stepped backward, away from my father. Butler staggered—he stayed upright longer than you might have expected—then collapsed without trying to break his fall and landed in the puddle he'd avoided earlier. My father leaned over him. The Dalmatians were playing, rolling and growling and thrashing a muddy rag. Butler squirmed under my father, his face pale and his eyes very wide, the back of his pink shirt soaked in mud. He tried to raise himself. But his knee was broken, bent to the side, and, seeing that, he stopped struggling and lay back, his hair sopped in the puddle. Then he began screaming. Just opening his mouth and letting out whatever shrill, jagged noises he could, and when that started my father turned and fled toward the stables, where I was supposed to be.

THE DALMATIANS HOWLED AT THE AMBULANCE'S sirens. We were loading the tack and horses into our trailer, and my father remained quiet except to tell me what to leave behind. The paramedics' voices and the rattle of a gurney made their way to our stalls, and Deidra Butler sobbed and kept saying, "Still here. He is still here." Butler cried out when they lifted him into the ambulance, again just some guttural noise, then came the sound of doors slamming and tires spinning in the mud and onto asphalt, then finally droning away. During all of this, my father worked as though the spectacle didn't concern us and everyone would benefit if we kept clear of the trouble.

We drove to a ranch farther outside the city, one nicer than Butler's and owned, I learned later, by the man who'd originally given my father the horses. A sign reading OLEANDER CREEK, HUNTERS AND JUMPERS hung over the entrance. My father left the truck idling while he negotiated with the owner inside the office. I climbed out and slipped sugar cubes to the horses, whispered to them through the trailer. White fences ran around the ranch, and the name of each horse was engraved on its stall—Texas Tuff Stuff, Johnny Boy, Madeline, Coffee Break. A covered arena loomed behind the stables, and a small girl was taking a lesson, giggling in her riding cap and boots.

Twenty minutes passed before my father returned. An electric gate opened and I sat on the tailgate to ride into the stables. He could secure only one stall that night, but another would open tomorrow, which suited him fine. He commented on how my mother could ride English style in the corral—something she'd never done at the Seahorse—but I couldn't recall her wanting to ride that way. My father asked if I liked the property and I said yes, because that was what he wanted to hear. Dusk blurred the sky as we unloaded and a lamp brightened near the stall, illuminating dust and other imperfections in the moist air.

"My thoughts feel focused now," said my father. We were driving home, and he started talking in the dark. "How are you doing?"

"I feel worried," I said. Then, a moment later, "Aren't you scared?"

My father chuckled and looked at me fondly, light in his eyes. "Boy, the only thing in this whole woolly world that scares me is losing you and your mother. I'd be in the tall grass without the two of you. I'd be in the weeds."

I didn't answer him. Outside my window the stubble fields looked like black water. My father braked at a stop sign, and the telephone lines buzzed above us. He cleared his throat, moistened his lips, then looked at me. "I lost my job today, Benny."

"Oh," I said. "I'm sorry."

We remained at the intersection, though for how long I don't know. There were no other vehicles around, and I began wishing my father would turn the corner.

"It's political, of course. It'll blow over soon enough." He rippled his fingers on the steering wheel, and lifted his eyes to the rearview mirror. Then finally he checked over his shoulder, and accelerated. "You're not supposed to know any of that."

"Okay. Does Mom know?"

My father shook his head, and after a moment, inhaled.

"About Edwin," he said. "It was reckless, I'm smart enough to know that. But the trouble's behind us now." For a moment, my father fixed me with his eyes—I felt him do it—though I didn't look at him, but stared straight ahead, watching our headlights shine through the night.

I said, "He didn't know what happened."

"He's no Johnny Straightarrow—remember that," my father said. I thought he would say something more, comment on the night or why he was out of work, but we did not speak again. Maybe he was allowing his mind to continue focusing, or maybe he felt he'd already said too much. He turned the radio on to a man singing opera, and although neither of us liked that style of music, we listened. I wanted to say something, though I didn't know what and so stayed quiet. My father seemed caught in his own thoughts, maybe absorbing the music or worrying about my mother or concentrating on something I couldn't know. Or maybe he was realizing that he'd crippled a man and that trouble was not at all behind us, but would be waiting when we rounded the curve of Longcommon Road and the lights of our small house came into view.

WHEN HE SAW THE POLICE CRUISER IN FRONT OF the house, my father said, "Okay, then. All right." He wasn't speaking to me, but just collecting himself before he parked near the curb and stepped out into the night.

My mother sat on the porch, smoking. She was wearing a terry-cloth robe, an old one I had not seen in some time, and her hair looked wet and recently brushed, tucked behind her ears. Our floodlights beamed down on her, making her look far away. Two policemen stood near her, one leaning against her Chevy and a shorter one in the grass, but when my father opened the door, they clicked their flashlights on and started toward him.

"Mr. Kelley? Mr. George Kelley?" the short policeman said. "I'm Officer Barrera."

"Are you fine, Marie?" my father called. "Are you feeling better?" The policemen and my father were nearing each other, but he was looking at my mother on the porch.

"I don't know what's happening now, George," she said. "I was in the shower." She shielded her eyes from the flood-light and leaned forward on her toes to see us better. Her voice sounded strong. A line of cars rumbled by on Long-common and my mother waited for their noise to fade before she spoke again. "Is Benny with you?"

"I'm here," I said. The taller policeman shined his light in my face. I was on the passenger side of the truck, standing in the dark street.

"Come here, Benny," my mother called, then in a lower voice, "Is that okay? Can my son sit beside his mother?"

"Sure," my father said. He was sliding his wallet into his pocket. "He'll do that just fine."

The three men stopped under our chinaberry tree, close to each other, as I walked to the porch. A wind blew that night, strong enough to rustle the leaves and make a set of chimes tinkle down the street. My mother grabbed my hand and squeezed it, then patted my thigh when I sat.

"I'll be with you soon." My father flashed a smile at us. "We'll clear this up in a hurry." Then Officer Barrera motioned my father toward the cruiser, while the other officer followed. And after that, they conversed in voices too low to hear.

Several of our neighbors had gathered outside, clustered on their porches. Occasionally a man's voice rose or a woman giggled or someone popped open a beer can, then everything would fall silent again and I felt people studying us in the dark. Through a window across the street, I saw a woman dancing on a television screen. My mother whispered that she recognized her, but couldn't recall the dancer's name. I expected her to ask me what had happened, but after a door slammed down the street, she tightened her bathrobe's belt and disappeared into the house.

My father spoke with the officers for some time. They frisked him. My mother hadn't returned and I appreciated her not seeing him bent over the cruiser's hood, his arms and legs spread. As Barrera patted him down, my father said something and the three men laughed. *They'll let him go,* I thought. But the taller officer took my father's hands behind his back and clasped the handcuffs on his wrists; there were no cars just then, and the click of the locks snapped like a ratchet. He continued grinning, as did the other officer, while they placed him in the backseat and closed the heavy door. Across the street, on the TV, the camera zoomed in on another woman's face, a singer, and inside our house, I heard my mother pouring a drink.

Soon Officer Barrera came up our driveway and smiled a smile to say he was sorry. The taller officer lowered himself into the cruiser—the interior light went on when the door opened and I saw my father in the backseat, adjusting himself so he wouldn't be sitting on his hands or hurting his elbows. The officer in the car said something to him, gestured with a pen, and for some reason I thought they were discussing me, maybe my riding or grades or my being an only child. Everything seemed very loud to me just then, each sound magnified—a dog barking on another block, the rope clanking against the flag-pole beside the mechanic's garage, the crickets trilling in my mother's flower bed.

"Ben, this is hard. I know." Officer Barrera flipped his tablet over. "But will you, please, to the best of your ability, describe the altercation between your father and Mr. Butler."

I watched my father in the car; he was staring toward the mechanic's garage across the street. It occurred to me that whatever I said would influence what happened to him, that right then the responsibility for our family lay with me, and he would want me to think in those terms—what became of us in the future depended on this moment in my life that felt like a dream.

I said I'd been feeding Colonel and hadn't seen anything. Barrera told me to estimate the distance from our stalls to Butler's trailer, so I guessed the length of a football field, maybe two. He positioned himself between me and the cruiser so I could no longer view my father, and I wondered about his family, if he was thinking about his own son as he spoke with me. Barrera resembled a fire hydrant, with a black mustache covering much of his upper lip, and I thought he could beat my father. He asked me where the horses were right then, and I admitted they were at Oleander Creek but added that my parents had been considering the move for some time. He jotted my answers onto his tablet and with each one he glared at me as though he didn't believe me, which, of course, he shouldn't have.

My mother returned then, dressed in shorts and a blouse. She covered her mouth when she saw my father in the cruiser. Officer Barrera handed her his card and said my father would spend the night in jail, and a clerk would call in the morning with more information. She asked if they served dinner there because he hadn't eaten since lunch, and Barrera promised to arrange a meal later that evening. Then my mother asked to speak with my father before they left and Barrera okayed that, too. It was around nine o'clock then, the night sky streaked with gray cirrus clouds, and most everyone had abandoned their porches and dimmed their lights. I guessed they'd seen my father get into the cruiser and could imagine for themselves what would happen next.

SLEEP CAME EASILY TO ME THAT NIGHT, AND THAT still surprises me. After the police took my father, my mother followed me inside and warmed the dinner she'd cooked that afternoon. We sat at our small table together, my mother and I, and talked, not about the stables or Edwin Butler but about regular topics, as though my father were working late and would soon waltz through the front door and our lives would resume. "Go to bed, Benny," my mother said as she cleared the dishes. "The sun will rise tomorrow."

She called someone while I readied myself for bed—I heard her dial the phone and say, "Hello. Okay. It's Marie," and the sound of a cigarette pack tearing open, followed by my mother's cough. Soon, though, she spoke in a soft, private voice and my thoughts drifted to Butler. I wondered where he was at that moment. My best guess placed him in surgery or possibly in the recovery room with his wife, who would be waiting for him to regain consciousness and ask what had happened. I sympathized with him. I thought of my father, awake in the night and in jail, punishing himself with words like *patience* and *restraint*. Then I fell asleep, and if I dreamed, I don't remember it, except that I slept well so they couldn't have been nightmares, just the uneventful dreams of a boy my age.

The hinges of our front door woke me. My first thought was that my father had returned, either legally or he had escaped, which made my heart pound. I dressed myself—just my jeans and shirt from the day before, no shoes—and crept into the kitchen. The lights were on, the radio played at a low volume. I checked my parents' room for my mother, and the bed was made but when I called her, she didn't answer. It was six o'clock, the time my father left for work on weekdays, so outside the air felt cool.

"They love popcorn," my mother said. She was kneeling beside the anthill. "I once owned a dog who liked it, too. Maybe we should offer some to the horses."

I only responded by nodding and putting my hands in my pockets, though my mother didn't seem to want a response. She had changed clothes since the night before, and wore now a gingham dress with her hair pulled back. I smelled a citrusy perfume.

"I used to kick their little piles and make them run around where I could see them, but not anymore." She raised her eyes to me, smiled, then looked back at the ants. "It's a change I've made in myself."

"That sounds good," I said. A van towing a trailer careened past.

"If you could change anything about yourself, what would it be? That's an important question." My mother crushed some popcorn in her hand, then sprinkled it over the ants. The concrete felt rough beneath my feet, cold. "And it needs to be something you *can* change, nothing like your height or the color of your eyes."

My response came quickly, as if I'd considered it often and had only been awaiting the question. "I'd like to be braver. I'd like to be less afraid of things."

"What a wonderful answer," my mother said, nodding. "I suppose that's inspired by your father." She stood and dusted the last of the crumbs to the ants, then clapped her hands together. Cars passed on Longcommon, their tires swishing over the asphalt, as though it were wet. My mother leaned over the ants again, then shouldered past me and sat on the porch. She lit a cigarette and sent the smoke through her nostrils. "I don't want to know what happened yesterday. Is that fine?"

"Yes," I said. "That's fine."

"Edwin's hurt, I know that. Your father is to blame for it, I know that, too." She closed her eyes and drew on her cigarette, held the smoke in her lungs before blowing it out. "The officer called about an hour ago and said they'd release him shortly."

"That's good," I said.

"Of course it is." My mother flicked her cigarette into our yard. Someone cranked a car's ignition down the street.

"These last few days," she said and stopped. She shook out another cigarette and lit it. "I haven't been upset over money. Or not having money. Your father can't believe that, but it's true."

"Okay," I said. "I believe you."

"I'm worried that when I die people will only remember me for my mistakes." The air in front of my mother became clouded with blue smoke, then the smoke spread and its scent wafted toward me. "Maybe I didn't pay Edwin. Maybe all of this is my fault."

"I don't think so," I said. My mother sniffled and touched the back of her hand to her eyes, then she looked at the sky, which wasn't special that morning, just hazy and slate-colored. Longcommon was quiet; the morning lacked the noise of wind or dogs or people whispering on dark porches.

"It's hard to know your parents. Both of mine had affairs." She glanced at me. "Can I say that in front of you?"

I nodded. It crossed my mind to tell her about my father being fired, but I said nothing. I wanted to protect my mother, but it was also easier to keep quiet.

"I knew my mother's boyfriend. He was their handyman, but he boxed on the weekends. A pugilist. She loved it, the fighting, and sometimes he showed her different punches or how to breathe through her nose. It was an art to her. My father hated it, though—said boxing was just violence, nothing deeper. Basic brutality."

"I didn't know any of that," I said.

"I wonder what you don't know about me." My mother smiled. "Who knows what we don't know? I wish I could remember the things I've forgotten." She stood up from the porch and dropped her cigarette, toed it out. My mother looked pretty with the sun starting to rise behind her and I liked being awake at that early hour. "Benny," she said, adjusting her dress, "think of all this as just violence. Maybe it's nothing more and everything will improve."

Then she stepped inside and left me alone.

WHAT I REMEMBER OF THE MORNING WHEN WE drove to take my father from the police station is only the sensation that we were loose from our regular lives, floating and spiraling away from where we had been the day before.

He just spent the one night in jail. Edwin Butler refused to press assault charges against him, so the police held my father for disturbing the peace and released him the following morning. They let him go without posting bond, just opened the doors and set him free. All of that confused me at the time, though it no longer does.

My father fixed breakfast for us after we arrived home from the police station, chorizo omelets and pecan pancakes the way he did on holidays. For much of the meal the only sounds were our forks scraping against the plates, or glasses being raised then replaced on the table. Gradually, though, my parents surrendered to conversation and by the time my father took our plates, he was making jokes and saying how he looked forward to bathing and washing the jail off his skin. My mother ran him a bath.

While she was out of the kitchen, he said, "Last night a man asked me how old I was." He was staring through the window behind our table. "And do you know what I almost said? Twenty-two. I had to stop myself. It's not something that has happened to me before."

I thought to tell him what my mother had said or to ask him about being arrested, but finally I moved to the sink and started soaping the dishes.

"The house feels bigger," he said. In the bathroom, my mother opened a cabinet, then she shut the door. "How was the old girl last night?"

"Not so bad," I said.

"Good," he said. He put his hands on each side of the window, leaned his weight against the wall. He exhaled. "Oh, Benny, there's a life ahead. We just make our way by the best light we have."

Then my mother called that the tub was full, and my father brushed past me. He thanked her for running the water and I heard them kiss, heard the floor creak as he stepped into the bathroom. I expected my mother to return to the kitchen, to sit at the table and smoke or drink coffee, though when I finished the dishes, she hadn't emerged from the hall.

The bathroom door was closed, but through it I heard the murmur of my parents' voices. My mother said, "That dirty Mexican" in a tight, hushed tone, and after leaning close to the wall, I suspected they were talking about my father having not eaten in jail, despite Barrera's promise. I pictured my mother sitting on the toilet, her legs crossed, while my father lay submerged to his shoulders in gray, sudsy water. And for a time, they were silent and I listened to cars swooshing by on Longcommon.

Then my mother said, "Oh, baby, that's okay. No, no, now. George, baby." Her words came quickly, but calmly, and although a minute passed before his sobs grew loud enough to carry from the bathroom, I realized my father was crying. I'd never heard that sound before. Maybe he'd told her about losing his job or about Edwin Butler, or both, or maybe he'd kept silent and his face just bloated and crumpled with tears. I imagined my mother leaning over the tub and embracing my father, pressing his wet hair to her breast, trying to still the heavy shudder of his weeping. It made me feel very young, younger than I'd ever felt in my life.

MEMORY IS MADE OF LOSS, AND SOMETIMES YOUR only hope is to recall that you've forgotten something you once knew, or thought you knew. If I ever knew why my father took me to the stables that afternoon, I no longer do. Maybe he thought he'd teach me something, maybe he only intended to talk with Butler and he believed his young son's future might benefit from watching two grown men negotiate a misunderstanding. Such considerations would have been within his character, but I distrust them. They come twenty years later, from a happily married, college-educated man who's never known violence. What I think, simply, finally, is that my father made a mistake.

We moved the horses into neighboring stalls at Oleander Creek the day my father came back from jail. My mother stayed home, napping. Setting up the tack rooms, I worried that my father would bring up Butler or Officer Barrera, but I also worried that he wouldn't. I wanted him to know what I'd told the police, wanted him to say that I'd done right by him and he was proud; I wanted him to thank me.

But he was quiet that muggy afternoon, quieter than usual. I asked him if he thought we'd keep the horses here for more than the month he'd paid for and he said, "If it feathers our nest." He was kneeling in the dirt, cleaning Lady's hooves, then he stood and started combing out her tail, then her mane. He gave me chores to complete—carry over the salt blocks, find nails whose heads or spikes stuck through the stable fences and knock them in with his hammer—but he said little else. He seemed wrung out to me, as if he'd been laid up in bed for weeks with an injury or illness, and now that he was back in the world, every small task exhausted his strength. Yet when the other owners started to arrive and walk over to introduce themselves, he rallied. His laugh was loud and generous, his handshake looked firm, his posture straight as a post; I'd never felt worse for him.

These were not the people from Edwin Butler's ranch. Their shirts were starched and bright, the rims of their hats were not crooked or lined with dust or sweat. They wouldn't think of digging a pit beside the corral and roasting a hog; they wouldn't come out to play all-night poker and watch over a colicky foal, and they would never let their horses hit more than a stiff gallop in the pasture. And although the men and women meeting my father seemed unaware of the differences between their lives and his, I think he noticed them acutely. I think their saucer-sized belt buckles were like mirrors for him, and he saw that he'd led his family into a different life, saw that we'd crossed a river and were wandering in an open field where we were as vulnerable as mice. Suddenly he knew he'd surrounded himself with people who could never conceive of doing what he'd done and not one person there would ever spend a night in jail. I tried to imagine myself being fingerprinted or raising my fist to another man, but I couldn't do it, and neither, I fear, could he.

But I wanted not to think of the future just then, only to hold tight that afternoon with my father and to stand between him and the life that would soon overtake us like a storm. I wanted to throw the saddles on the horses and ride, to prove to him that I was still there and all was not yet lost.

"Here you go," I said once he and I were alone in the stable again. Other owners would show themselves soon, so I wanted to seize the opportunity while I could.

I extended my hand, his rings warm in my palm. They'd been in my pocket since the day before, and I had slipped them on and off my fingers countless times and I had been bothered by how even the smallest was too big for me, even on my thumb. My father seemed surprised, though not necessarily happily surprised, to see them. He'd given the rings to me when he had known he'd wind up in jail, but I suspected he'd not thought about when they would be returned. Maybe depending on his son in this way was insulting or humbling or liberating or confusing. Of course he eventually took them back, but he didn't do it right away. I said, "You forgot about them." He laughed a little then, which made me feel that I'd betrayed something about myself, my youth or optimism or how little I knew of him. We stood in the hot stable for a long, long moment, my arm growing tired of holding out the rings and him looking at me suspiciously, as if I might be tricking or trapping him, luring him to reach for something that I would only take back at the last second.

Outside the Toy Store

WESLEY WILSON FINALLY DECIDED TO APPROACH Anna because she looked weary. Sitting on the bench with her purse in her lap and her eyes closed, Mrs. Anna Eichhardt seemed diminished, no longer alluring or charming or dangerous; she was stripped down in a way he'd never seen her. She appeared heavier, too, and he imagined she would hate him seeing the extra pounds. This was in San Antonio, the weekend before Easter, and the wind cutting through the open-air mall still stung and smelled of the benevolent winter. "Anna," Wes said in a small voice. Then he stepped closer and cleared his throat. "Anna?"

She didn't recognize him immediately. Behind her, a line of parents and children waited to meet the Easter Bunny, and with all of the shoppers passing in front of her, she seemed unable to focus. Then her eyes lit and her hand flew to her mouth. She said, "Well, my God."

They embraced, quickly, timidly, like two friends' spouses. It had been five years since she'd told him she couldn't compete with his dead wife and sick daughter. He was thirty-nine, wearing a new scarf, a coat, shined shoes, and a wool suit purchased specifically for the managers' conference that weekend. The suit flattered him, and he saw Anna seeing that.

He said, "I saw you in the toy store and wanted to say hello."

She squinted, her hand lingering near her lips. She said, "Oh, sure, of course. Hello, hello!"

Anna tucked a lock of hair behind her ear—a nervous habit he recalled and anticipated a second before it happened. He slipped his hands inside his coat pockets and shifted his shoulders. The flow of shoppers had inched him closer to Anna. To someone passing, he thought they might look like parents conspiring about what presents to buy for the holiday.

He had left the hotel when the meetings adjourned, intending to walk to the strip club he'd found the night before. But the chill had bitten into him, so he'd ducked into the mall for a scarf and coffee. The plush giraffe in the toy store window had caught his eye and he went in to look at it—Rae, his daughter, had always loved giraffes. And inside, Anna was kneeling between two small boys, buttoning one of their parkas. He could almost make out her voice through the rustle of bags, the hurried conversations of shoppers. Though he'd never seen the boys before, he was sure they were her sons, and they kept him away, just as her husband would have. He followed the three of them into the courtyard and watched the boys sprint to join Anna's sister in the Easter Bunny line. Anna sat on the bench, and Wes assumed her husband was absent that afternoon.

Over the years, he had considered contacting her, had even dialed her number and hung up after hearing her voice, or her husband's, but because he never saw her, he convinced himself that she had moved from the city. The thought of her absence comforted him. Now, sitting beside her on the bench, he told her about the promotion that had brought him up from Corpus and to the conference, and his hollow voice irritated him. He said, "I spoke on in-store promotions."

"How exciting," she said, her eyes smiling. Anna wore a long black coat, square-toed boots, and tight gray gloves. Everything looked expensive. She said, "Is the bookstore crazy as ever?"

"People still steal Bibles. We lose more of those than any other title."

"Gosh," Anna said. "I remembered that the other day. That always made me so angry." She crossed her hands in her lap, and in the tight gloves they looked like a child's.

In line, the boys circled their aunt's legs, trying to hide from each other. A movie theater loomed behind them, and a teenager wearing a red bellhop suit blew into his hands under the marquee. Anna said, "I teach and freelance now. It keeps weekends clear, which is nice."

Probably Anna's nice weekends entailed her husband, Gordon Eichhardt, driving the family to their lake house, where the boys splashed in the shallow water. Wes pictured the lake house as a cottage with tall windows and wicker furniture, and he had imagined it that way since Anna and Gordon Eichhardt had claimed only to be colleagues at the Chamber of Commerce—"the Chamber" was what they used to call it. It had intimidated him then, and it intimidated him now.

But he also could tell that she liked sitting in the mall with him, even though she was probably wondering why he was in a toy store. It was that the store's brightly colored displays and music box noise always moved him in ways the cemetery did not. Occasionally he was tempted to buy a doll or stuffed animal and arrange it on Rae's shelf, but more often he simply admired the toys, puzzled over those she might have liked. It seemed natural. He worried the day would come when he could no longer return to her in his mind, when he would find even her memory gone.

But for now the memories still came without his bidding, sometimes in mists, sometimes in storms. As if in premonition, just before he'd seen Anna, here in the mall, he'd remembered Rae finding a frog and calling her outside. It was the day he introduced them to each other, and already they were holding hands. Wes was pulling crabgrass in the sun. Rae stood a few feet from the frog, leaning forward but refusing to step closer. She'd said, "I'll get Buster."

"Honey," Anna said, "Buster doesn't like frogs."

"They can play together."

"Frogs and dogs don't play. They're different. But we'll name him. What's a good name for a frog?"

Rae touched her hospital bracelet, one of her first. She'd called it jewelry. "Daddy," she said. "His name is Daddy."

Anna looked at him, then Rae did, too, pointing at the frog. Her mouth made an O; light came into her eyes. "What a perfect, perfect name," Anna said. "He *does* look like your daddy."

Now on the bench, Anna touched his arm. "Wow, Wes, I can't believe we're sitting here. I'm delighted, truly, but doesn't it seem strange?"

"Yes, it does," he said. "It does a little." Behind Anna, her sister tousled one boy's hair. They couldn't be older than three. He asked if they were twins.

"They are." Anna leaned closer, and he smelled the warm, earthy scent of her hair, the same scent he used to find on his pillows. He worried she might smell the strip club on him, smell the dancers' body lotion on his coat.

"Robert, on the left, is the talker," she said. "And Franklin—he's, well—he's shy."

"I'm sure he'll grow out of it."

Then Anna said, "When they're sleeping, I can't always tell them apart. If one of them scratches his nose or something, I notice differences. But not when they're perfectly still."

"That's normal. I'm sure—"

"Wes, you look fabulous," she said briskly. In five years, her voice had acquired an East Texas rasp and lightness. It sounded, in a way, seductive. Briefly he imagined stealing away with her into a darkened vestibule or fitting room, though they'd never acted so boldly when they were together. Under Anna's clothes, he remembered, her skin was a soft shade of amber. Then he wondered whether Gordon Eichhardt might be buying toys while Anna distracted the twins; perhaps he might be watching or approaching right now.

Anna said, "Did you recognize me at first? Have I changed?"

"You look a little different—not much, though."

"That's nice to hear. I gained weight, of course, but I still like to swim. I guess I always will."

"I remember that," Wes said. Then he heard himself ask, "Do you ever think about that time in our lives?"

"Sure I do. Just the other day I remembered the night we danced in your bedroom. A Tuesday—I'll always remember that because it seems romantic. Dancing on a Tuesday. Buster kept scratching at the door."

His memory opened, and he felt himself plunging helplessly into it. He almost told her about the car hitting Buster, but controlled himself. There seemed some kindness in staying quiet. He said, "It was nice, wasn't it?"

"Oh, yes. Yes, indeed." She seemed refreshed now, no longer forlorn and fatigued. She said, "But when I recall it, I don't hear a song. I remember the candles, your chin on my shoulder—you hadn't shaved—and how slow we moved. Was there any music?"

"I don't know," he said. "Maybe we played the stereo."

Anna smiled, a furtive, oblique smile that made him realize he'd been wrong. She wasn't heavier at all. This was the same woman from that night in his bedroom, when, among candles, they swayed with the smooth, languorous movements of bodies under water. Rae lay in bed, weak and exhausted, but still under a small umbrella of hope. Dancing with Anna that Tuesday without music, he almost proposed, almost whispered the question in her ear, but he refrained, because holding her, he divined the dark way all of it would end. When he told Anna he loved her, he meant *You'll leave me, too.*

In the mall, neither spoke for what seemed a long time, a time long enough for Wes to see that Anna was still beautiful; Anna would always be beautiful. He made a motion to stand up from the bench, saying, "I should let you go."

"What about you, Wes? Do you ever think about us?"

"Yes," he said. "Sometimes."

"Then tell me something." Anna's voice softened. She smiled, and Wes leaned forward, rested his elbows on his knees. She said, "Tell me what you're thinking right now."

On the morning after he had left the hospital for the last time, he called Anna because he'd promised to, but also to shock and punish her, and to hear her apologize for leaving him. After the funeral they spoke a few times, always with tears and remorse and words waiting to be pulled from wherever they exist before the voice. But she never agreed to come back, and he began deploring her for it.

"You can tell me," Anna said. She glanced at her boys, then turned back smiling. She looked young and lovely and strong.

He said, "I hope it never happens to you."

"What?" Anna smiled and squinted, as if given a compliment she hadn't understood. The bellhop opened the exit door from inside the movie theater, wedged a doorstop under it. The mall noise sounded like a waterfall. Anna said, "You what?"

"To Robert or Franklin," he said. "I hope they get a fair shake in things. I hope they never get sick, and I hope they grow up to have grand lives like their father."

"Oh." Anna sucked in her cheeks. Her eyes hardened. She said, "Oh. Okay, then. Is that why you followed us? Is that what you wanted to say?"

"No," he said. "I don't know. There's a lot I want to say."

"Maybe next time, then," Anna said. "Right now I need to stand with my children while they meet the Easter Bunny. You do whatever you want. Leave or sit here or do anything except come near me. I don't want to see you anymore."

She took her purse from the bench, but the bag gaped open and some of its contents spilled onto the bricks. She closed her eyes and exhaled loudly. And when she didn't move, Wes suddenly regretted approaching her. He despised everyone who saw her purse dangling from her hand, and he crouched to begin collecting what she had dropped.

"This has nothing to do with you," Anna said. On her knees, she started jamming items into the bag. She reached for a lipstick that had rolled under the bench, but only knocked it farther away. Again, he thought they would look like a husband and wife.

She stood and brushed off the front of her coat. She said, "And I wish I hadn't told you about the twins sleeping. God, that makes me feel so gullible."

It sounded as if she wanted to add something, maybe that her marriage with Gordon Eichhardt was splendid or that he had divorced her or that over the years she had called Wes and been too afraid or ashamed to speak. Or maybe she would say that in her worst moments she *had* imagined losing the boys, but God forgive her, she had seen a life for herself on the other side. She could have said anything. Though finally she said nothing at all, but just turned her back to Wes and left him alone on the bench.

The mall had become crowded with the audience from the theater, a rush of people that momentarily impeded Anna's path, and he watched her wait for them to pass. She checked the time, then looked at the marbled sky and ran her fingers through her hair, her beautiful hair. On her first opportunity, she cut through the crowd and disappeared. Only then could Wes stand and leave. The wind was colder on the street—it made his clothes feel heavy and wet—so he raised his collar and started toward the strip club. Already the encounter seemed far behind him. His life felt unchanged. In fact, the idea of change hardly seemed a possibility anymore. Maybe that was why he'd approached her at all, to incite a drama that could open a new door, or an old one, but the effort had failed. Such impotence, however, didn't bother him; he'd lived through worse. Walking with his face turned down from the wind, he wondered if Anna had remembered the day she met

Rae. Probably she had. And some of that memory probably stayed with her as she found her boys in line. While they spoke with the Easter Bunny, Anna's sister would ask what Wes had said, and Anna would efface the question to deny him even the distant satisfaction of riling her again. She would smile. She would reduce everything to a short, insignificant encounter—or perhaps, even worse, a pleasant encounter—with someone she used to know, someone she had not at first recognized.

Corpus Christi

DRIVING TO BAYVIEW BEHAVIORAL HOSPITAL took Charlie Banks half an hour. The sand-colored facility stood ten miles outside Corpus Christi, among wheat fields and grazing pastures. He drove a leased Lexus and liked shifting into fifth on Rodd Field Road, an abandoned straightaway where he could open up the engine. His top speed was 120 miles per hour. He'd bragged about this at the office, though he didn't say where he was going. Edie had called the car pretentious, but Charlie viewed it as evidence that they were finally hitting their stride.

Bayview was nowhere near the bay. The surrounding area was staked with sun-bleached signs advertising acreage for sale; besides the hospital, there was only one gas station, a Kum and Go. ("Why not call it Kneel and Blow?" Edie had said the week before. "Why not Ejaculate and Evacuate?") Four shaggy-trunked palm trees anchored the hospital's empty parking lot; the place resembled a deserted country club. A man in fatigues stood outside the automatic doors, swigging from a leather flask. Military men always seemed to be at Bayview, loitering with wheelchair patients, littering the entrance with cigarette butts. Nurses and orderlies smoked with them, too. Charlie made quick, kindly eye contact, then went inside, registered, and took a seat across from a woman holding a motorcycle helmet. His stomach grumbled; he'd forgotten to eat lunch. Soon the soldier entered, trailing a cloud of viscous June heat into the air-conditioning. Charlie flipped through a magazine, the same one he had looked at yesterday, and tried to quiet the fear that some calamity had befallen Edie since they'd spoken that afternoon. Maybe she'd cribbed some tranquilizers or carved her wrists with a shard of broken mirror. He opened his eyes wide and considered hustling out for a candy bar, maybe a tabloid and pack of cigarettes for Edie. But anything he brought in would have to be x-rayed and quarantined before she received it, so he stayed put.

The woman hugged the helmet, swinging her leg like a pendulum. The soldier sat beside her. He said, "Another five minutes."

"None of this makes sense to me," she said.

The soldier crossed his arms; his biceps bulged. He said, "Plenty of people in that boat."

"When we were young, a plane crashed behind our house," she said. "Donnie and I were outside and got covered in soot. Mother always worried it traumatized us. Maybe she was right."

"I doubt this has much to do with a plane."

The woman shrugged, as if there was still a chance that whatever had happened could be explained away. Charlie suspected someone close to her had died. She was young, with fleshy arms and a faded dolphin tattoo on her calf. Keeping quiet seemed a chore for her. Edie had been that way for a while. The woman looked forlorn, which he also understood.

What Dwana Miller was thinking was that she needed to pull herself together. She'd been frazzled all day. First she'd gone to trade shifts at the Yellow Rose, in Southport, but once there she realized this was her weekend off. Then she sped from Southport to the naval base, parked at the infirmary and rushed in, remembering too late her brother's message about being transferred to a civilian hospital. Outside, her keys hung in the ignition of her locked car. Her purse was there, too, with the cookies and comic books she'd brought for Donnie. *You stupid shit,* she'd said in the parking lot. *You stupid little shit.*

Now, in the waiting room, she said to the soldier, "I guess they'll make him quit the Army."

"Discharge."

"Doesn't that sound too hard, like he's a spy?"

Just as he realized he was staring, Charlie found himself fixed in the soldier's gaze. He smiled apologetically, then glanced through the window. A chain of seagulls was flying back to the beach from the landfill. The Lexus sat alone in a row of parking spaces. The car still thrilled him. Before the Lexus, they'd owned a little Ford that Edie called Fido because the old landlord had forbidden pets. That was in Dallas. She was thirty-four, two years younger than Charlie. When the law firm in Corpus called to offer him their network support position (the salary so high he thought they were joshing him), Edie flat refused to move. She liked her job (fund-raising for nonprofits) and liked living close to the nursing home that her mother's dementia had transformed into a grand hotel. He argued that they could buy a house and travel, perhaps find a hospital for her mother down south, but she stonewalled him and he began resenting her. Then, after two years of trying, Edie was pregnant, and he saw an opening and let reason shine through. He said, "Corpus would be a great place to raise children."

That was hardly a year earlier, but in Bayview, and after the miscarriage, that life seemed as far off and turbid as the floor of the muddy, olive-tinted bay, which you couldn't see.

DWANA WISHED SHE'D TAKEN A CAB FROM THE naval base. But because unauthorized vehicles were prohibited past security, and because some documents (Donnie's, no doubt) needed to be delivered to Bayview, the infirmary attendant had suggested that Omar escort her to the hospital. She hadn't known he rode a motorcycle, nor that he'd feel compelled to wait while she saw Donnie. Nor had she figured how, later, she would get into her locked-up car or, for that matter, home. *One disaster at a time,* she thought.

They sat alone in the waiting room, twenty minutes before it would be time for visitation. Whiskey on Omar's breath, a wet-smelling musk. Maybe she'd seen him at the Yellow Rose; Army boys ferried over on weekends, and after working there two years, she recognized them everywhere. She wanted a change. She'd considered beauty college in San Antonio, but more recently she'd entertained notions of a clown school in Houston. An advertisement had promised work at parties, hospitals, schools, even rodeos. How easily she pictured herself painting on heart-shaped eyes, tying balloons into wiener dog hats. She would run the idea past Donnie, amuse him. And she'd tell him she was sleeping with her boss's wife—"What else is new?" he'd say—a woman who two nights before had asked Dwana if she'd ever done a *taj mahal*; she'd meant ménage à trois.

"Me and my boys are shooting pool later," Omar Delgado said in the waiting room. "Always room for one more."

"You have children?"

He squinted, smirked as if being fooled. "Oh, no. Buddies, fellows from the base."

She forced a smile, feeling stupid. She wanted to check the time, but resisted. "A lot of fun I'd be."

"Might feel good to relax." He'd been at her since they'd arrived, angling his thick neck so he could meet her eyes. He said, "And you don't have to worry about driving home."

"It looks like I've already handed over my keys."

He laughed, then a silence settled. With the quiet came the memory that had resurfaced since Dwana heard that Donnie had been arrested. She is eight, he is six, playing in the sorghum field behind Mema's house. He wears a plastic fireman's helmet, carries a kite that refuses to fly. He sees the plane first, a crop duster wobbling in the air, tendrils of smoke billowing from its tail. *We should be on the ground,* she thinks; *our heads should be between our knees.* But they stand, she behind him, touching his shoulder. The plane flies low enough for her to see the pilot's goggles, his mouth moving. No. No goggles, a backward baseball cap, and he's wiping his eyes furiously. Then the ground buckles like a sheet snapped taut, and she runs into Donnie in a haze of smoke and pesticide.

"You don't look much alike," Omar said. "You and Don."

"I usually hear the opposite." Not true; no one ever compared them. She had dingy hair and blue eyes, her father's; Donnie's eyes and hair were black, shiny. For years she'd dreamed about the plane; he had, too. Their dreams were never nightmares, which seemed odd.

"Southport's a peach of a town," Omar said.

"It's where you're either drunk or fishing. They say that at the bar."

"Like I said."

She imagined serving longnecks in a rainbow wig and red squeak-ball nose.

He asked, "You got a sweetheart over there?"

"No, just a husband," she lied.

Omar'd had enough of this flaky woman. He went into the parking lot for a smoke and a pull from his flask. The sky was hard, heat shimmering on the baking asphalt. A broken line of seagulls flew east from the dump; their shrieking sounded like a baby crying. Soon the line would fill in, hundreds of birds weaving their way back to the island. He picked a piece of tobacco from his tongue. A flash of a memory: Papa spitting tobacco juice into the sand. Maybe he *would* call the boys tonight. He'd drop the cook's sister at the base, shower and change clothes. Or maybe he'd swing by Sandra's first, let her wonder about this white woman behind him on the bike. A Lexus turned into the parking lot. A doctor's car, he thought, but the driver was too nervous-looking, a jittery man who had trouble activating the alarm. Probably a banker or a salesman, someone you met once and never saw again.

DONNIE MILLER DISLIKED CARD GAMES, BUT THE monotony of poker in a psychiatric hospital was oddly relaxing. And the other patient, Edie Banks, was enjoying herself, so he didn't mind spending the afternoon this way.

He'd arrived at Bayview after two weeks in the naval correctional facility—the Army had no such facility on base—to undergo tests and counseling before the arraignment. He had arrived in handcuffs, escorted by MPs; he'd just turned twenty-four. Everything had started because of a comic book; no, everything had *ended* because of it—*Incredible Hulk,* No. 181, near-mint condition, worth two hundred dollars. A birthday present from his sister. He'd shown it to everybody and explained its value—the first cameo appearance of Wolverine, a haunted mutant who forever changed comics— but they'd been hoping for a girly mag. Most were Donnie's age, lascivious, spring-loaded men who wore dress khakis to the Fox's Den on weekends. They called him queer and knocked over the water bucket whenever he mopped; on the soda machine someone had scrawled, *DM sucks sloppy cock.*

Watching Edie Banks put down two pair, he recognized a tenderness that made him want to please her. She reminded him of an old woman for whom he should open doors and speak loudly. She was in her thirties, sun-freckled, rusty-haired; she wore dental braces. She resembled Dwana's child-hood friend Joanie Mahurin, a dewy-eyed girl who'd paraded around their house in panties. A tan line on Edie's ring finger, perhaps that was the problem. Perhaps her husband had stepped out on her, as Donnie's own father had. Maybe not. None of it mattered. Already he understood that none of it mattered.

He hadn't been looking for the comic book, but noticed it missing. He looked in places he would never leave it, under his bed, in his duffel, behind the lockers. Of course they'd taken it, probably Buford, the wiry, fawn-skinned ringleader. Yet upon finding Buford in the rec room, the comic's cover folded as if he was enthralled by the story, Donnie felt briefly relieved. Two others played darts in the room, but they paused when he entered. Buford said, "Found your book."

Then they were behind him, holding his elbows, while Buford tore pages. The deliberate, excruciating noise of paper ripping. Donnie yelled. The screaming scorched his throat—he tasted the gritty texture of his own windpipe—and he was five years old again, grabbing a dogwood branch with a mud dauber on it. Instantly pain shot from his palm through his body, like broken glass in his veins, and he surrendered to it. He woke swaddled in crocheted afghans; his mother and Dwana worried that he was going into shock. The memory came and went in less than a beat, then the rec room returned and he broke free as simply as slipping from a shirt. He stomped one of the men's feet, felt the metatarsals snap; he elbowed the other in his solar plexus, heard him heave and collapse. And now Buford was pinned against the paneled wall and Donnie pushed a dart to his jugular. The soda machine droned beside them—*DM sucks sloppy cock*. The smell of menthol, Buford's recent shave; under his jaw, a swatch of missed whiskers. Blood dripped from his mouth, and although Donnie didn't remember striking him, he knew he must have, so he did it again. Cracked his forehead against the bridge of Buford's nose.

Then the not unfamiliar thought: Maybe he was queer. Maybe only queers would notice the curiously beautiful light in Buford's eyes, the hazel-flecked green, or the pleasing woodsy scent of his hair. He felt every inch where their bodies touched, pressed his weight harder against him, pushed his groin against Buford's thigh. The contact neither aroused nor disgusted him. Buford was mumbling, whispering because his throat was blocked, but Donnie made no sense of the words. He raised the dart to Buford's mouth, parted his plump, tight lips; he heard them unstick. Blood-smeared teeth, pink-white gums, bubbles of thick crimson saliva. He pressed the dart's gold point to the corner of one of those gorgeous eyes, caressed the skin, grazed the edge over his lashes. "You like that, don't you?" Donnie heard himself say. He slid the dart into one of Buford's nostrils, pushed it against his septum. A needle into a stubborn cushion. A stake into wet ground.

"I'm kicking your butt," Edie said in the hospital. "Full house."

"You're a card shark," he said. "I'm, like, a perch."

"My mother used to play on Sundays. Maybe I got it from her. She lives in Dallas. She thinks she's a grandmother."

Confused, he arranged the cards.

"She has Alzheimer's. I've never told her I miscarried."

He shuffled the deck, wishing he could do it more quietly. A flyer on the wall advertised a seminar called "Preparing for the Unexpected"; another invited patients to join the Bible study/weight loss group. *Are you thin enough to fit through the pearly gates?*

"I send her framed pictures of babies from magazines. Does that sound calculating or cruel?"

"No," he said, though maybe it did.

"Those were my husband's words. He's a stickler for the literal truth, for facts."

He dealt the cards. By the patio door, a retarded man named Lester Riggs rested his forehead against the window. Probably he was watching the one-eyed cat that some people called Lucky. Others called him Jack.

"I decided to have a girl. I named her Esther, after my mother." Edie studied her cards. "Are jokers wild?"

"Yes, I think so."

"Charlie's a keeper, though. If we were stranded on an island, he'd fashion a raft out of twigs. That's his character. I'd sit in the sand crying."

Edie drew three cards. Donnie held a pair of sevens, and a flare of excitement bloomed in his chest, his fingertips. He thought he might win.

"When I got pregnant, he was so excited he couldn't sleep for a week. I had to mix tranquilizers in milk. He never learned to swallow pills."

Donnie laid down his cards, hopeful until Edie fanned out three jacks. He averted his eyes to Lester, who stood marching in place. Outside, a car alarm sounded, then chirped off, then started again.

"Charlie's mother left his family for a nudist cult in Arizona," she said. Then she cackled. "Listen to what I'll tell a stranger. Maybe I *am* a nutso."

The MPs had put him in a padded cell on base—he hadn't known those really existed—and listed him on a suicide watch. He sat cross-legged in the middle of the room until morning, conjugating verbs in his head—Latin, Italian, Spanish, French. He never slept or spoke or moved, just to prove whoever was watching wrong.

THROUGH THE WINDOW THAT SEPARATED THE WARD from the common area, Charlie watched the nurse knock on a door. He felt suspended and vulnerable, as if life could unravel if she had to knock again or twist the knob herself.

Then, release: Edie peered out and said, "Oh, it's Charlie." She padded down the corridor in her terry-cloth slippers, loosing her hair from a ponytail.

Charlie was surprised again to realize how she thrived here. The daily arts and craft classes—she made stained-glass (plastic) hearts—and the stray, one-eyed cat in the garden suited Edie as nothing had for a year. The same with the nightly bingo games, the book and cake-decorating clubs, the high school chorale that performed every Thursday. A juggling magician named Crazy Paul would visit over the weekend. Yesterday she had said, "We're ecstatic. It's like he's one of our own."

Brightly colored tables crowded the cafeteria, the long, light-filled room where visitations took place. Twelve-step posters lined the walls; reinforced windows overlooked a dry, blond pasture. The starchy smell of dinner—meat loaf? pizza?—lingered, and he considered sneaking a waxy roll from a tray to quell his hunger. The woman from the waiting room took a seat near the window; probably the soldier was outside again. Edie had staked herself at a yellow table near the far door, and approaching her, Charlie tried to gauge her spirits. Maybe sitting at a yellow table connoted more emotional stability than sitting at a blue one; he didn't know. His only thought was: *She's here.* When he reached her, she said, "Guess who's coming home Monday."

"Fantastic." The word tasted hollow. He'd expected her stay to be prolonged, more therapy scheduled, more lithium prescribed. He said, "Everything's waiting for you, right where you left it."

She smiled—her braces stoked his guilt, made him want to apologize—then she waved as a nurse ushered another patient into the cafeteria. Heavy, fortyish, wearing thick lenses that clouded his eyes, the man had the pale, doughy features of Down syndrome. He stopped at the soda fountain and nudged the lever until an orange stream showered his hand.

"You need a cup, Lester," Edie said.

Lester laughed, affecting a chagrined surprise for forgetting his cup again. Charlie hadn't seen him before. Edie watched him fondly, as she watched children. Lester ambled to the window and pressed his fists to the glass, rocked to and fro. She whispered, "Lester the Molester. He points at women's crotches and says, 'I know what that is.'"

"Points at you?"

"Oh, my knight. No, not me, but I've seen him."

Maybe she was lying, but he avoided pressing anything, especially here. He felt scrutinized by the nurses, cowed by what they understood of Edie that he didn't. He worried about sending her over the edge again.

"How's home? Is the nest still there?" Edie asked.

Earlier that year, a mother sparrow had nested inside the mailbox. Charlie had thrown out the dense, sod-smelling tangle of reeds and branches, and Edie called him a bastard and refused to eat for two days. When the nest reappeared, she slid bread crusts into it and made the mailman leave letters inside the screen door. How many times Charlie had caught her listening for hatchlings he didn't know. Now he realized he'd forgotten to feed the bird as Edie had instructed. He said, "We're all there, ready to roll out the red carpet."

A young, acne-pocked man entered the cafeteria, and the woman from the waiting room ran to embrace him. Lester snapped his head toward them, then shifted back to the window. The woman started crying; the man rested his chin on her scalp.

"That's Donnie," Edie said. "He lets me win at cards."

"Why is he here?" Immediately, Charlie regretted asking this. The question assumed people had to do something, or not do something, to be hospitalized. So far, he'd acted as though Edie's stay was routine, precautionary. "Like an oil change," he'd said that first night, trying to cheer her. He acted this way for both of their sakes.

"I think he beat someone up. Savagely."

Donnie appeared incapable of causing damage, more like someone who'd been bullied all his life. He had a jittery manner that would invite cruelty. Charlie had pitied such boys in his youth, while he himself usually slipped under everyone's radar, avoiding altercations and attention of every kind; most days he still felt invisible. What could people surmise from Edie's appearance—a thirty-four-year-old woman in wrinkled pajamas and braces? Maybe she seemed a person who'd lost her footing but now, rested, was fit to leave. And maybe she was, but Edie excelled at showing people what they wanted to see. How many times had they gone to parties where she interacted famously, then at home collapsed on the bed, too distressed to say good night? Not to mention the business with her mother. Esther called from Dallas at all hours and Edie narrated a sunny, alternate life in Corpus. Charlie had refused to indulge the fictions, and when he overheard their late-night talks, his stomach roiled.

Now he tried to remember ever seeing another visitor get a soda. He thought anything in his stomach—a handful of cereal or a cold slice of pizza—would sharpen his wavering concentration. Edie fingered the salt shaker, then rested her palms on the table. She said, "We talked about it today. In my session."

His muscles tensed, and he felt himself—not his arms or body, but everything inside—recoil. Edie wouldn't look at him. She ran her tongue over her braces. He said, "How did it go?"

"Sometimes I imagine the weight without trying to. It's like after swimming in the ocean, then a week later you still feel the waves."

This didn't sound like Edie, and he was trying to make sense of it when she said, "Let's leave Corpus for a while. The doctor suggested I reacquaint myself with the world."

"Sure," he said, automatically. Then, suddenly, unexpectedly, he was eager, awash with a grateful, poised energy; his nerves tingled with the unmistakable electricity of hope. "We'll start planning on Monday. I'll talk to travel agents."

"Maybe to a desert. We can bathe in sand like Hindus. The new nurse told me about that."

"Anywhere at all." He liked the tone in his voice, the tone of an actor in an important scene. Perhaps a week in Bayview *had* rejuvenated her, absolved her of that debilitating uncertainty. *How easy,* he thought, *to underestimate the wounded.* Donnie and his sister laughed behind her; this also pleased Charlie. Lester moved from the window and tapped the lever on the soda fountain again, but pulled his hand away before getting splashed. He did it twice more, then buzzed for the nurse. Edie waved again. Charlie did, too, confidently now, flaunting his wife's renewed devotion.

Lester snickered, pointed at the nurse: "I know what that is."

LEAVING THE HOSPITAL, CHARLIE FELT JAZZY. Hope and vigor always returned after a visit, and accelerating past the split-rail fences tonight, he vowed to harness his replenished optimism; X-ray or no X-ray, tomorrow he'd bring her a tabloid, flowers. Stands of live oaks and bowed willows were silhouetted along the road; the Kneel and Blow's sign flickered in the distance. He cranked up a Tejano version of "Brown-Eyed Girl" on the radio and gathered speed through the humid, heathered dusk. He imagined nights in the chilled desert and wondered how different the sand would feel from the beach. His stomach no longer ached; he would cook at home. The speedometer crested ninety. He floored the accelerator. He sang, though he knew no Spanish.

He recognized the helmet and caught a clear look at the woman's face; she stared south, unaware. Yet the familiarity of the woman and the soldier and motorcycle relieved him; steel and glass and a solid deafening thud, but nothing like this could be happening with two people he'd just seen. He knew he could be killed but knew he wouldn't be. *I'm wearing my seat belt. Hindus bathe in sand.* The hard-hitting noise became everything, he tumbled and flailed inside it. A peculiar softness to the collision, too, as of pressure released. The bike's handlebars twisting like rubber; the passenger window breaking so quickly, so completely that thinking no window had ever existed made perfect sense. The Lexus slid. The seat belt constricted. The man said, "Agárrate! Agárrate bien!" The motorcycle flipped. Everything stopped.

Glass covered the seats, jewels in the moonlight; the showroom where he and Edie priced engagement rings. He didn't remember steering off the road, but he was parked on the narrow, crushed-shell shoulder. Lightning bugs flashed, the memory of returning to the jewelry store the same afternoon, fearful that he would forget which setting she'd preferred. Now, moving terrified him, but moving seemed tantamount to surviving, the first in a series of actions that would reveal themselves necessarily. He lifted one arm, then the other. Bent his knees, rotated his ankles, swiveled his wrists; slowly he twisted his neck. No air bag had inflated. Why? Because the car had been broadsided? Smoke poured like liquid from the hood. The air reeked of scorched tread. Though the passenger side had suffered the impact, he expected his door to be jammed and was surprised when it opened easily; this seemed bolstering, promising. He'd slipped the ring on her finger while she slept, and when she woke the next morning, she said yes.

The night was hushed, darkening. Everything felt askew and surreal, as if he'd slipped through a gap in time's weave and all he'd known about himself was unrelated to where he was now. As he walked in the glow of taillights and gauzy moon, his legs and mind were hollow. He expected his knees to give with each step. The oily air smelled of horses, cattle, manure. "You've had an accident," he said aloud. Insects whirred and clicked in the leaves; electricity sizzled in power lines. He expected voices, figures clamoring to ask if he was hurt. He paced fifty yards with only errant glints of broken reflectors on the asphalt, shards of plastic that might have been there for months. Perhaps he'd hit a deer or coyote, had suffered a head injury that spawned hallucinations of bending handlebars.

Then, near a tangle of mesquite trees, his breath left him. Had he not been watching the ground, he would have tripped. The soldier lay on his stomach, feet pointed inward, arms splayed. Charlie felt in a vacuum; the noise of the night rushed back in waves; he could no longer discern individual sounds. *There was a stop sign,* he thought. *They came from the west, they went somewhere after Bayview.* Over his shoulder, he glimpsed the Lexus—he'd not closed his door and light spilled out. No sign of the motorcycle or the woman or anyone else at all.

"Hello," Charlie said. "Hello?"

He surveyed the area. Trees, sky, moon, ground, the lone gas station two miles ahead; each where it should be, each becoming another affirmation. Something rustled in the leaves, then the sharp, resonant cracking of a single branch. His heart pounded. He waited for the woman to appear, but the rustling quieted. Whatever was there was gone. He placed two fingers on the man's neck and waited for a pulse. He'd never done this or ever imagined doing it. A quick thumping under his fingers; no, *in* his fingers, his own heart deceiving him, beating throughout his body. Edie knew CPR, had campaigned unsuccessfully for him to take the course with her. The flesh was grated and pulpy. He worried he pressed too hard or too soft, pressed the wrong place. Nothing. He found his own pulse pumping under his jaw, then tried the soldier's wrist. A raft of clouds moved across the moon, turned the skin a luminescent gray. The air became pungent, earthy. Closed eyes, open mouth, cracked-out teeth. Charlie had to shut a memory from his mind—Edie saying she wanted braces, wanted to laugh without covering her mouth. He choked back vomit. The pulse would not come. He waited another few minutes, afraid to stop waiting. Eventually, he stood and walked on.

PAPA AND MAMA AND THE NEW COLLIE, OBO, ON Malachite Beach. Only in Corpus half a year and already Papa's located the best fishing spot—trout, sea bass, grouper, redfish. Aluminum lawn chairs; a Styrofoam cooler full of tamales and Fanta and Schlitz; Obo barking as Papa levers himself from his seat; the smell of Winstons and Hawaiian Tropics oil and the tonic in Papa's black, black hair.

"Give some slack, Omar."

He releases the line, though he wants to reel in. His arms tremble, his heels dig into the sand, granules between his clenched toes, and a sudden wind scours him. In school he's learned that melted sand becomes glass, that mirrors are windows with one side painted black. Fourth grade, a bully has made him touch, with one outstretched, humiliated finger, his flaccid, brownish-purple penis.

"Now take him in, *un poquito*. Don't fight." Papa is excited, proud.

Omar reels. Two seagulls hover motionless overhead. Behind him the earsplitting roar of a motorcycle, his mother calling Obo, the dog scavenging in the washed-up detritus—sargassum, a dead Portuguese man-of-war and cabbagehead, mangrove pods. They bought Obo a month before. She was listed in the paper for $75.00, OBO; he'd believed it was the dog's name, which made his mother laugh through her nose, so Papa coughed up forty dollars. Obo sleeps beside the door, but Omar hopes she'll start jumping into his bed.

"Leave off, Junior."

He will tell the whole school about the fish; Papa will tell his Thursday-night poker players; Mama will fry it; he will sneak Obo the skin; she will jump into his bed. The fish thrashes on the hook. Omar fears the line will snap and all will be lost, for suddenly existence itself depends on not bungling this. He offers more slack, this seems right, but Papa spits tobacco juice onto the sand and says, "Agárrate! Agárrate bien!"

EDIE WAS FOUR MONTHS ALONG WHEN THE NURSE called Charlie's office. He'd been waiting for the security desk to buzz when she arrived, though he'd thought nothing when an hour passed. Probably she was dallying in a fabric store. They had only the one car, Fido.

He took a cab to Spohn Hospital, acted stoic and amenable toward the driver, as if a purposeful composure could improve the circumstances. His breathing tightened. What his mind latched on to was the nursery—the antique bassinet bought at an auction, Edie's ongoing search for the perfect hanging mobile, the picture books she'd started collecting. That she spent most of her days working in the room while he'd barely set foot in it turned his stomach so quickly he feared he'd throw up. Last week she'd had paint in her bangs—did she still? He imagined Edie exiting the freeway and being rear-ended and sent into oncoming traffic. He imagined the doctor waiting until he arrived to break the news about the pregnancy. Streaks of sweat tracked down his arms. The cab seemed stalled in traffic, even speeding toward the hospital.

She was leaning against a soda machine, talking to a nurse. No wheelchair, no bandages, no hovering, grim-eyed doctor. She seemed a visitor. "Fido got run over," she said, smiling. "I think we have to put him to sleep."

In bed that night, he picked up the joke again. "I'll miss the old boy."

"He's out of his misery."

"He'd want us to move on, to stay strong."

At first she seemed to be laughing, then he realized she'd started weeping into his shoulder. She said, "We've won the lottery, Charlie-boy."

Two weeks later, they woke on sheets soaked in blood. In his memory, Charlie always believed the thick, mealy smell roused them. An ambulance came, and within hours she'd bled so profusely that she had to have a hysterectomy to save her life.

DWANA HAD THE ILLUSION OF FLOATING. THE CROP duster, the pilot's mouth moving; Donnie on his back, balancing her stomach on his raised feet, her arms extended like wings; the crystalline image of Omar Delgado's hands, though not really his, but her first lover's, a boy named Billy Mahurin; in a lifeguard stand, he predicted she'd eventually have perfect breasts; the moon coloring the beach cobalt, a pack of coyotes tussling in the water; she told Billy, "Donnie writes in four different languages. I never understand his letters."

Billy crouched beside her in the dark. They had just finished and lethargy overwhelmed him. She felt gravely embarrassed, disappointed and mystified, worried he was judging her against other girls. She couldn't stop blabbering. She said, "He waited a long time to say his first word. Then one day he just blurted, 'I want a banana.'"

Billy said, "Are you okay there?"

"I'm wet." What a wonderful answer! The prospect of hearing how he'd volley back after being inside her was exquisitely terrifying, like swimming after dark or riding a motorcycle.

"There's been an accident," Billy said.

Not Billy at all; though the voice sounded familiar. From the hospital—Donnie is in Bayview. Billy is married or a father or dead, so much more than her first lover now, and she is beside a road, a pewtery night in Corpus—she *had* ridden a motorcycle!—the high pitch of mosquitoes, the moist scent of cow shit.

"I know," she told the man, but that was silly; she hardly knew anything. "Are people hurt?"

"I'm not sure," he said.

"I'm just a little cold."

Billy again, suddenly and completely; he removed his shirt and tucked it around her arms. She lay on her stomach, his touch shamefully comforting. She said, "Perfect."

"We'll sit tight. We'll catch our breath, then decide what to do."

"It might have been Omar's fault," she heard herself say. "He was speeding. And drinking. We'd seen my brother at Bayview."

"Did you go somewhere after—"

"They'll expel him, the Army will. I never wanted him to enlist."

"My wife is there, too. He lets her win at cards."

In the lifeguard stand surrounded by coyotes—a pungent yet not unpleasant odor of wet fur all around—Billy and the man were both present. No ocean, though. The water had evaporated. She thought to scream this news, but the men seemed unalarmed, so no need to worry. She said, "He's just a baby. He used to be afraid of water. I don't know what he's afraid of now."

"That's okay," the man said. "He's safe there."

Billy and the coyotes vanished, as if spooked. She thought to say *Poof,* but asked, "Why is your wife in the hospital? Is that rude?"

"No," he said. "We lost our son."

"Oh, Lord," she said. "Lord, Lord." Her inclination was to prattle on, but she knew to hush. This man's wife had auburn hair and braces and a sad, dramatic jaw; she looked like Joanie Mahurin, Billy's sister, the first woman to break Dwana's heart. The man and his wife had sat near the soda fountain—who knew what they whispered? To know them, to understand who they essentially were, you only had to know what they'd lost. This was explicitly clear: Everyone could be seen that way.

"How cold are you?" the man asked.

So, he stayed afloat by changing the subject. Good for him.

"We should find Omar," she said. "I'll help. I'll sit up."

"Wait—"

"I feel a little mixy. No. Woozy, that's the word. I guess that's normal. I don't feel broken anywhere."

"That's good news."

"I don't want to see Omar," she said. She'd thought they would return straight to the base, but he'd detoured behind Bayview; he slowed in front of an A-frame, revved the engine until curtains parted in a kitchen window, then he popped the clutch and rocketed into the darkness. She said, "I wouldn't mind him being scared. Maybe his bike got crashed up."

The whine of sirens. Sirens coming to the field covered in glaucous green smoke, like fog; sirens coming to the lifeguard stand while she and Billy grope for clothes, she has his pants, he has her bra; sirens coming for Donnie as if he'd killed someone.

"The cavalry," she said. "Omar probably called them."

"Good," the man said, turning away. "At least we know he's all right."

THE MORNING BEFORE THE DOCTOR COMMITTED Edie, the stink of cigarette smoke woke Charlie. As his eyes adjusted to the sunlight splashing into their bedroom, he fantasized that they had guests—a wife from the firm or a neighbor. Edie had quit cigarettes for the baby, but he knew it was her, knew it as surely in bed as when he found her at the kitchen table in front of an overflowing ashtray. She said, "I'm smoking again."

She looked older than she was, a sullen, accelerated aging that he'd noticed other mornings, but today it seemed permanent, not nascent wrinkles that would smooth with a shower and coffee. A beat before he saw them, he remembered her new braces.

She said, "I sneak out at night. I use mouthwash."

Their recent days flashed through his mind, a blur of filmy heat tinged with Listerine. She said, "Are you going to interrogate me, or can we just skip to my punishment?"

"What happened?"

"Interrogation it is."

"Honey, I just want to help."

She stayed quiet, a worrisome, irritating silence. He felt he'd been lured into dropping his guard when he should have seen this coming. He remembered that he only called her Honey when she bottomed out; he couldn't stop himself.

"I don't see how you do it, Charlie-boy."

"Edie . . ."

"You work, you socialize, you zip around in your hot little car."

"Honey, let's not—"

"When you were talking me into it, do you know what I kept waiting to hear?"

He did know; she'd said it before.

"'It's a great place to raise children.' I thought you'd say that about the car."

"I got a car, you got braces. We're not so different." As he said this, he wished he hadn't.

She nodded, once. Her expression suggested he'd incriminated himself, though he couldn't yet see it. Her cigarette had burned out. She had trouble lighting another one, as if aligning herself in a mirror where her movements were reversed. He reached to help, but she leaned back.

"I took some pills last night. Or this morning, I can't remember."

His heart went flat, his mind blanked. "How many?"

A disgusted little laugh sent smoke sputtering from her lips. "Apparently not enough."

"I don't understand," he said, though he did. She had him cornered, and they both knew it. He noticed a bowl of pancake batter on the counter, cracked eggshells on a paper towel, the skillet on the unlit burner—a project that had proved too formidable. Those dishes, their air of defeated optimism, leveled him. There was nothing he could say now. He squeezed her hand, but it remained limp as raw steak. As cool, too. She lidded her eyes, then tears hung on her eyelashes, dropped to her cheeks, the table. *Her mother*, he thought. The phone had rung late last night, and even asleep, he'd understood Esther was asking about the baby. Maybe contriving details had finally sapped Edie. And at once he understood his role. He knew to speak calmly, blithely, to call the doctor. He knew she was in no condition to stop him.

Hanging up, Charlie said, "He'll see us right away."

"What does he want to see?"

"Just a checkup. He'll run tests, then tell us where to go from there."

"*Us?*" she said. "He'll tell *us* to go to Bayview, then he'll tell *you* to go home."

YEARS LATER, AFTER EDIE LEFT BECAUSE HE reminded her of all she'd lost, Charlie would see the night as nothing more than coincidence, a series of circumstances that made sense in dim, regrettable lights. He'd remember a feeling of buoyancy, a survivor's euphoria, the subdued thrill of escape. Maybe such stability had been false at its core; that was not how life happened. Or maybe because it seemed so shatteringly absurd, it was exactly how life happened.

An ambulance had arrived on Rodd Field Road, then a police cruiser. Paramedics fitted the woman with a neck brace and backboard, laid her on a gurney and hoisted her into the ambulance. When one of the men asked her about Omar, Charlie mouthed, "She doesn't know," and the subject was dropped. The medics worked with fluid, satisfying efficiency, passing Charlie's shirt back to him while adjusting dials on monitors while discussing coyotes with the woman. Soon another medic—three now, though he'd first believed there were only two—directed him toward the police cruiser. His heart stuttered, his throat constricted; *arrested*, he thought. But he only needed to sign forms verifying that he'd declined their advice to go to the ER.

During all of this, he worried he'd not done everything he could for Omar, that he'd not waited long enough for breath, that the young soldier still lay suffering, praying a more competent soul would realize a sliver of life hadn't faded. Maybe all of this should have burned like hope, for if he were still breathing, maybe he could still be saved. Soon, though, a sheet covered the body like a mound of clumped snow. How strange to think: snow in Corpus. The sheet hovered in Charlie's peripheral vision, regardless of where he turned. The officer

asked questions, and though Charlie couldn't admit to speeding, he answered as thoroughly as possible. He told about visiting Edie, about seeing the woman and Omar at Bayview.
When he finally confided about Omar's drinking, he went
under a wave of relief. Perhaps the officer went under, too; perhaps he'd already found the flask. A wrecker came for the bike,
another for the Lexus. The sounds of the night amplified—
soughing wind, whispering fields, lines of far-off traffic. Another ambulance came for the sheet glowing in the moonlight,
and the officer drove Charlie home, Patsy Cline in the speakers.

At home he drank bourbon; it seemed the thing to do. The
whiskey relaxed him; was this how Omar felt, steering into the
Lexus? Without realizing it, Charlie had turned on every light
in the house. His hunger returned and a light-headedness set
in, but he didn't eat. He sat at the table for another hour, doing
exactly nothing, while the desire—the *need*—to talk with
someone manifested itself. He felt pieces of the need gravitat-
ing together until they formed a complete thought: *Call someone.* Of course Edie came to mind, but with her came the
improbability of negotiating answering services and nurses,
convincing someone to wake her. Wait, then; let her rest. The
same hesitation with the woman. He'd have to persuade the
hospital staff, but that would be complicated by not knowing
her name, nor even to which hospital she'd been admitted. His
mother or father, a partner from the firm? He dismissed everyone. The night moved around him like mist.

The phone ringing. His mother-in-law, Esther, sneaked
into the hall of the nursing home. When he told her Edie was

in bed, she sounded affronted. A moment later, she asked, "How is Dallas this time of year?"

"Corpus. We moved. *You're* in Dallas."

"I can't wait to see you," Esther said, unfazed. She perpetually thought they were visiting the next weekend; Edie always told her they were. "I haven't spoken with the girl lately. I get worried, I worry something's happened."

"She'll call soon."

"The ragamuffin's wearing her out, I guess." She laughed. This was a grandmother's compliment.

Charlie walked to the window, feeling dizzy. He pictured Esther huddled in the hall, her body folded over by osteoporosis but ready to bolt if an orderly rounded the corner. She wheezed. When he'd first met her, she'd been a member of a power-walking group, five widows who pumped around shopping malls before the stores opened. That she would never spend a morning that way again felled him. She'd toiled for two decades in a dry-cleaning plant, then hawked Tupperware, then she started getting lost in parking lots, wandering off in her nightgowns; she had told him that Edie learned to roller-skate behind a Catholic church. Suddenly the last thing Charlie wanted—it seemed the one abuse he couldn't endure—was for Esther to hang up.

The window was beaded and streaked with condensation. He said, "I'm looking at little Esther right now. She's sleeping. I have to whisper."

"Yes, don't disturb her." Esther had lowered her voice, too. Outside, June bugs batted off a streetlamp.

"Do you know what we've started calling her?" His voice surprised him. Then before she could answer, he said, "The little bug."

"Oh, she's a beautiful bug. I show her pictures to the nurses."

He knew her eyes were wide, her hands jittering with local tremors. When he'd signed the forms for the medic, he couldn't stop his fingers from shaking. His name came out spidery, illegible.

"Esther, I want you to hear her."

"Oh, Charles, would you?"

"Listen. Listen to your granddaughter," he said and extended the phone into the air.

He'd always expected a rift to divide his life, a meridian by which he would measure before and after. Now he realized that no such divisions existed, just a steady letting go until you found yourself in a place you never thought you'd be. In an ambulance or nursing home, in a psychiatric ward, alone. More than ever he wanted to call Edie. He'd wanted to call since the morning they found blood on the sheets, for her to pull him to her breasts and console him. She had invited this, but he'd never been able to oblige, never would be able to. He thought to take one of her sleeping pills, but remembered they were all gone.

He raised the phone. The line stayed quiet. He thought Esther had left the receiver dangling to hide from an orderly. Again it seemed he'd concocted the whole ordeal, that he only needed to dislodge this waking dream before it gained purchase in his mind. The veneer was thinning, though, like the night, and soon everything would be visible, undeniable.

"Esther?"

"Isn't that something?" she said after a moment. "The little bug snores."

IN LESS THAN A MINUTE, THE NEW NURSE—JASPAL Janecki, two weeks on the job, left momentarily alone and more afraid of her patients than her superiors—would knock urgently on Edith Banks's door and take an unprecedented, probably job-endangering chance to ask her to sit with Donald Miller; his sister was unconscious at Spohn and he'd asked for Edie. A strangely clarifying swirl of pride and despair would spread through her, a bracing call to arms that tingled in her cheeks and scalp. But the nurse hadn't yet knocked, and Edie lay in bed, Ambien-drowsy and about to remember the crabs.

She had loved Corpus, loved it. The house, too. A two-story Victorian on Brawner Parkway, hardwood floors and a porch in a quiet neighborhood half a mile from the marina. Four bedrooms, theirs and a spare, one for Charlie's office and one to convert into a nursery. She visited the city's few museums—small, but lovely places to pass time, to bring children—and she drove over the causeway and watched men fish. She started a diary. A satin-covered notebook filled with details of the pregnancy—she had become farsighted and her sense of smell had intensified; she could no longer abide grilled food—that she would eventually present to her daughter; though they had decided against an amnio, she always considered the child a girl. She wrote that eventually she wanted to volunteer at a library or day care, get involved with PTA. She wrote of driving around in Fido: *Fido is our car.* Or she wrote about staying home. How she opened the windows and let the balmy breeze ventilate the rooms; how she sat on the porch—*I'd always wanted a porch and now we have one!*—with headphones on her stomach, playing Mozart.

She had always known she'd be a mother, had known it more surely than she'd known she would ever marry. Fear had vanished. There was anxiety, but not doubt, not melancholy. She hoped the girl got her eyes, but not her rusty hair or bunched-up teeth. She wanted her to have Charlie's confidence, his bounding, resilient verve. He was like a boy, really, industrious and easily dazzled, deadly serious and short-sighted; how many nights had she reminded him to eat, to stop picking his nose while he read? Years before, she'd filled out a survey that asked how your partner would react if stranded on a deserted island; she'd answered that he would build sand castles. But he'd become a stand-up father. In the mornings he slipped her feet into socks before they touched the floor; he handed her scissors handle first; whenever she was going to the beach, he set out sunblock, shades, a floppy hat.

The beaches—Mustang Island, Padre Island, Malachite—were often deserted in the late mornings, her favorite time to go. An occasional surfer or fisherman, a boy riding a horse or an older couple combing the shore, but usually she was alone, listening to the waves roll and slosh. She hunted for sea glass and shells among the dried kelp, the barnacled driftwood. Once, she'd carted home a bag full of small rose-and-mahogany-striped conchs and soaked them in bleach overnight. When she woke the next morning—her body still craving its first cigarette but settling for water and a grape-fruit—a dozen alien-looking hermit crabs were scuttling around the table and floor, down the ladder-backs. Wake Charlie? No. She gathered the crabs in a shoe box and left him a note: *Gone to fabric store. Love, E.*

Why lie? Because he would worry.

The island was abandoned. The sky, like the water, was mother-of-pearl gray, the air unseasonably brisk, poised. She set the box halfway between the scruffy dunes and played-out waves, unsure which would be best. The crabs stayed so still she feared they'd suffocated. *Whoops,* she thought. Finally one stirred, then another and another; then they all came alive. Some were spindly and slow, some so swift and graceful they seemed to swim in the air. Maybe this gave her the idea, or maybe she remembered having always wanted to, or maybe no idea formed at all and she acted on perfect compulsion, in-stinct. She undressed. She waded out, holding her newly swelling belly. Her nipples tightened, the water cut into her calves, thighs. Elegant waves formed and broke beyond the outer bar, sand slipped and shifted and collapsed beneath her heels. She'd read about a child who'd misunderstood *under-tow* as *undertoad,* and feeling the riptide's far-off, indifferent tug, she wondered if all children misunderstood this, if hers would. She pictured an amicable cartoon frog, fat with as many good swimmers as bad ones, setting up a picnic in the deep. Her teeth chattered; she couldn't stop smiling. Then she ran, bounded into the breakers and screamed and giggled in a widespread, beautiful lightness, a maternal ecstasy. She turned and surveyed the sweeping, sinuous shore beyond the heaving waves. The sea oats feathering the slope of the sand, a rickety lifeguard tower in the distance, the mouth of a trail leading into the tawny dunes and the limitless mystery they promised lovers, children. Mystery? Yes, mystery. There was a shadowed life here—the sand dollars inching just under the mud flats; a pocket gopher nibbling the roots of magenta morning glories; the diamondback basking in the sun; the coyotes still damp-coated from slinking in the tide; the crabs claiming new shells; the scissortails prancing among the laughing gulls just about to take flight. Who knew where they'd land in an hour, next year? She only knew where they were now, with her, only knew her life was becoming more than it had been. *Here we are,* she thought. *Here we are.*

The Widow

HER HUSBAND KISSING HER CHEEK, THEN STEP-
ping outside and scooping the dog into his arms. How
tenderly he lowered him to the truck seat, how nonchalantly
he set the pistol on the floorboards before driving away into
the night. The dog was a miniature black poodle named Peppy,
and Richard had owned him since before they were married.
Peppy's muzzle was silver, like his paws. He had cataracts and
he'd not eaten in days.

She lay in bed when her husband returned. She heard him
wash with the garden hose, then enter the house and creep
into their bedroom to unload his pockets onto the dresser.

"Where's your shirt?" she asked, then before he could answer, "Oh."

He sat on the bed, pulled off his boots. She touched his
back.

"Where?" she said.

"A field off Yorktown. A cornfield that's just been plowed."

"Did he—"

"Minnie."

"How much would a vet have cost?"

"Oh, I think the old boy deserved better than that."

He'd said this for a week, though she knew he also wanted to save money. Overtime had been slim lately, and they were seven months pregnant. In bed, she could smell the dark field on him, a cloying scent that promised he would handle such things. She whispered, "Are you okay?"

He stayed so quiet she thought he was weeping, or about to. He who never wept, he who always calmed her when she fell to pieces. She wanted him to cry, though.

"Honey?"

He said, "My ears are still ringing."

MINNIE MARSHALL DIDN'T SLEEP THE NIGHT BE-fore arranging her funeral. She stayed up in the den, smoking and watching television and applying a mud mask. Her foot kept time with the ceiling fan; September in South Texas. She thought of when they buried Richard, of course—thought of the long line of mourners, the poem Lee had read. She hadn't known he would read anything—hadn't even known he wrote poetry. Would he write one for her?

Before he returned home to care for her, Lee—thirty-three, unmarried, renting the bottom floor of a house in St. Louis and writing his dissertation on an obscure, utterly forgettable historical subject—had taught high school history. She had liked telling people this. Yet, lately, she often thought of him as the boy who'd run screaming from butterflies, as the infant who some nights would quiet only when Richard shredded rags beside the crib; the ripping noise awed him. Or she thought of the year he'd been stricken with rheumatoid arthritis, when they spent days watching game shows and soap operas or, if his knee felt strong, going to the pond and tossing crumbs to ducks. The ducks had always cheered him. She had known him best then. High school and college seemed waves that knocked him away from her; or his girl-friends were the waves. Of all of them, she could only re-member Moira, the bawdy, patchouli-smelling sister of his friend Russell, who rarely wore a bra. After his father died, he'd visited more, but he remained distant, a guest who spoke only when spoken to. She'd learned not to pry on those short stays but imagined that prolonged time together would foster conversations, wear thin his reticence. Now, home for a year, he seemed never to have unpacked his bags; he seemed to have layered himself in silence like winter clothes.

Some mornings she allowed herself to make a racket to rouse Lee sooner, clanging pots or dropping spoons into the sink, but today she let him sleep. She felt croupy and belea-guered. She brewed coffee and thumbed through the *Caller-Times*. When Lee had lived in Missouri, she'd sent him articles from the paper and she still sought out stories to interest him. Always she saved the obituaries for last. None of today's names were familiar, neither from the cancer center nor from life before. The sunrise was opening the kitchen. She mixed batter for waffles, beat eggs, fried sausage. Normally Lee ate cold cereal, but she hoped a solid breakfast might start the morning right. The cooking took an hour and she had just sat down when he began stirring. Her heart quickened. She took her ashtray from the table. Smoke bothered him while he ate.

He said, "You can stay."

"Get 'em while they're hot," she said. Slowly, she brought a heaping plate to him. If she rushed, or forgot to pause after standing, she found herself light-headed and reeling, then on the floor, hearing Lee's frantic voice as he rushed to her. She fell often, far more often than he knew.

"Did you sleep well?" he asked.

She sipped her coffee. "Wonderfully. How about you, sweetheart?"

"I thought I heard you walking around last night."

"I wanted some chocolate," she said. "I drifted off watching a show about France."

He nodded and resumed eating. As in his youth, he still cut food with his fork rather than a knife. He mixed ketchup into his eggs, stirred sugar into his coffee. He sopped syrup and sausage grease with his toast. She loved watching him eat.

"There's more of everything," she said.

He shook his head, still chewing, and rose to rinse his dishes. He returned the ashtray. "How do you feel?"

"Full of energy," she said brightly. She lit a cigarette. "I thought we'd go to the pond after the appointment. We can get sandwiches for a picnic."

He smiled, even laughed a little, and looked at her as if she'd suggested sprinting to Houston. Probably he'd expected her to complain.

"Have you taken your medicine?"

She held smoke in her lungs, then blew it over her shoulder, away from Lee. Sometimes she lied about taking her pills and spent the day worried he'd catch her, but this morning she behaved.

"All done," she said. Then after a moment, "More cars are broken into at funerals and weddings than anywhere else. People forget to lock their doors because they're too emotional."

He set a ceramic bell on the table. The bells were all over the house. She would ring one if she fell, or felt pain or had trouble breathing, or if whatever was coming for her came and she couldn't bear to face it alone. The bells comforted Lee and shamed her.

She yawned.

"You should nap before we go. Or I can reschedule."

She waved her hand—pshaw. She asked, "Do you know what the French used to call the guillotine?"

"A little early for beheadings, isn't it?"

"The widow."

He swept crumbs into the sink. A jolt of guilt for not washing the breakfast pans stung her; she could almost remember washing them. In Lee's presence, she was acutely aware of tasks she'd not completed. She said, "Daddy spent some time in France before I met him."

He braced himself. No one else would have seen his inward tensing—a quick, despondent inhalation, as if she were about to drag him under water—but she noticed. The water was talk of his father. She doubted that Lee avoided the discussions because they depressed him—rather, he thought they grieved her. And they did. What she couldn't explain was how she loved talking about Richard, adored hearing his name. She felt happiest in those unforeseen moments when she turned and for an instant, thought she'd seen him; when she woke still believing he lay beside her.

She said, "My traveling days are over."

"Mama . . ."

"I wasn't going to say that." She snuffed out her cigarette, then tried lighting another, but her lighter wouldn't immediately spark. She said, "Traveling just seems such a hassle now."

"You'd like France," Lee said. "When a person lights a cigarette, he offers everybody one."

LINDA "MINNIE" MARSHALL WAS FIFTY-FIVE WHEN the doctor said cancer. Her boys were both gone. Richard—husband and engineer, taker of early retirement package, reader of mysteries and griller of lobster—had died six years before; Lee had lived in Missouri since college. She worked as an accountant, owned a late-model Oldsmobile, and lived in the three-bedroom house the life insurance had paid off. She had seen the doctor because she'd been more tired than usual—her potassium was low again, she'd guessed. The exhaustion could have been a blessing; her body could have finally been adjusting to a life alone, settling into a routine without the boys, and if she honored the change, her days might bring her happiness again. If not happiness, at least less sorrow. But the doctor had sat heavily on the rolling stool, removed his glasses, and outlined options for treatment. Because he gave her a fair chance for recovery, she knew she would die.

She had considered not telling Lee of the disease, had considered letting it run its course untreated. He would be cowed by the diagnosis—she knew this as surely as she knew his name—and he would not understand how it could come as a relief. For years he'd beseeched her to move beyond his father's death, and now, finally, she would. Then, unexpectedly, she was mortified and needed him home. She needed his company in the chemo ward, needed to see him when the oncologist pressed the stethoscope to her back or pointed to X-rays where the tumor in her lung glowed like a star. She needed him to interpret what the doctors said; she told him she didn't want him to censor the information he got from the doctors when he talked to them alone, but he lied anyway and she knew it. When she asked him about the flashes of color in her peripheral vision, pinwheels and splotches and starbursts, he blamed the sun or tricks of light. When she asked about her ruined handwriting, he claimed to see no difference. When she asked how long she would live, he said you couldn't trust doctors.

Dressing for the appointment took over an hour. Breakfast had drained her, and now she was winded doing her makeup, weak-legged as she slipped into her skirt. Every button was a chore. How perfectly easy it would have been to stretch out and shut her eyes, but she pressed on because she'd already canceled the meeting twice. She thought to take a nerve pill, but decided against it; she was bleary enough. For years she'd rushed to dress for work and get Lee to school, and now she wondered how she'd ever managed. A wave of pride rolled inside her. The doctors had said her memory would fail, and often she'd forgotten what she tried to re-member, but the unbidden past returned vividly. The musky scent of Richard's hair gel; the sequined fabric she'd sewn for one of Lee's Halloween costumes; years later, the noise of him and a girlfriend in the shower, thinking she should be angry, but really feeling pleased; the mower still idling on the after-noon she found Richard in the half-cut yard; the thought thirty minutes before, *I bet he's thirsty*; the grass clippings on the glass of water she'd brought him. The memories assailed her, asleep or awake. She wore them like pearls.

Lee drove because she no longer could. She swerved and veered, sped and stalled. Twice she'd gotten lost a mile from home. Both of them blamed her medication, but she knew the pills were not the problem. Now she rode in the passenger seat, checking herself in the mirror. Half-circles hung under her eyes; her face was gaunt and pale. Her makeup looked rushed. Her hair, though, was full-bodied and healthy. After the treatments, it had grown back thick and dark and lovely, another woman's hair.

"I feel like we're going to a museum," she said. "We're all dressed up."

Despite the desiccating sun and humidity, she wore heels and a long-sleeved satin blouse. The sleeves hid the bruises that dappled her arms; the softest bump scarred her. Also, she was always so cold now.

Lee said, "Too spiffy for ducks. I vote for lunch and a matinee."

"We can change clothes. I'll want to sit in the sun after this."

Then a thought occurred to her. "But don't dress me like this, okay? Just jeans and a T-shirt. Sneakers. No makeup."

"Okay, Mama."

"And no jewelry. The morticians steal it."

Lee adjusted the rearview mirror. As with talk of his father, he refused to discuss her dying. Yet she needed him to know these things. Because she'd botched the past year of his life, she strove to spare him her burial. The dementia would set in soon. No one had said that outright, but she saw it coming. Poor Lee. Listening to her babble and watching her body falter, feeding her soup and waiting, waiting, *waiting* for her last breath would be torment enough without fretting over her jewelry and car, her house and clothes and last wishes. In the recliner at night, she devised ways to slip information into conversations, but the ideas evaporated with the sunrise. Her ideas were dew and mists.

"The last time I wore this, Daddy took me to *The Nutcracker*," she said, though suddenly the memory seemed slippery, possibly completely wrong. "Nothing like that had ever come to Corpus. He bought tickets for Christmas. Your father looked dashing in a suit."

"And you look fabulous in red," he said, glancing at her blouse. "You should wear it more often."

That she would never again wear the outfit was palpable in the car, and she waited for the feeling to disperse. They passed a corner where people sometimes sold puppies from truck beds, but none were there today. She hated the dogs being sold that way, but their absence always disappointed her.

"Here's a test," she said. "What was in Dad's car when I met him?"

Lee shook his head. Richard had strolled into the office where she worked as a receptionist. He wore a tweed jacket, a full beard. She had said *Just a minute,* had said it in an abrupt, frenzied tone that made him chuckle, and he'd started calling her "Minute." By the time he left, he was calling her Minnie, and it had become her name.

"A poodle," she said. "A little black poodle—I could see him through the window. Isn't that something?"

He smiled at her.

They rode beside the bay, coppery light glimmering on the marbled water. She said, "Isn't the weather gorgeous? We can walk a trail at the pond."

"You *are* feeling good."

She wanted to say "Fit as a fiddle," but suspected the words might wound him, so she checked herself. And now that he'd acknowledged her energy, she was momentarily relieved of the charade. She was an actress between scenes, out of breath and nervous. Her heart raced. Outside, the blurred horizon seemed close enough to touch. She remembered going to the pond during chemo, Lee's hand on her elbow as she stepped over the exposed roots of live oaks. Now, he turned a corner and the sun blinded them. He lowered both visors, but she pushed hers back up. The heat felt glorious on her battered arms.

"Daddy used to fix pancakes for his poodle on Saturday mornings," she said, lighting a cigarette. "His name was Peppy. He died before you were born."

THE MINISTER BEGINNING THE LAST PRAYER OF the service, Minnie regretting Richard being on a diet when he died. She wished she'd been able to cook for him that last month, to prepare one of her recipes he loved. What it would've been, she had no idea. Just as she had no idea how she would survive life without him.

Lee folded the sheet of paper with his poem on it and slid it into his pocket; she heard the paper crease.

Richard would have said she'd spent too much on his funeral—as he'd always said about the Christmas presents she bought—and they would have argued over the receipts at the kitchen table. He'd always meant to plan his funeral, to save her the trouble and prevent her from spending what she'd just spent. He was fifty-eight, and wet grass had kept bogging the mower. He'd said he would come right in; they were going to a movie that night. She hadn't cried during any of this, not in front of anyone, not even Lee. She was proud of that. Maybe Richard would have been proud, too.

"Amen," the minister said, raising his head and opening his eyes.

Shrimp, she thought. *He might have wanted my fried shrimp.*

IN THE FUNERAL HOME, NOW, WITH LEE, SHE wanted a nerve pill more than ever. The high ceilings and tall windows and Spanish tile floors made her anxious. She sat on a plush couch while Lee registered with an old woman behind the reception desk. How the woman stood it, Minnie couldn't imagine; how the water trickling in the stone fountain didn't drive her mad. Behind her, heavy oak doors opened into the chapel, and down the hall were viewing rooms, the refrigerated floral displays. All of it nauseated her; she fought off a shiver. A slow, tinny music whispered in the speakers. Among the headstones, you could hear and smell the ocean, less than a mile away, but inside there was only the incessant gurgle of the fountain, the smell of frozen flowers.

"Won't be long," Lee said.

"That's a lousy thing to say."

His eyes shut, a short exhale. "You know what I mean."

She rocked forward and straightened his shirt, something she'd done all her life; just then it seemed she could list every instance. She said, "Look at your collar. We can go shopping after our picnic."

He leaned back, his standard response. "How do you feel?"

"Tense," she said. "They'll try screwing us into every little thing."

"Let's hear what they say."

"They'll say, 'The more you spend, the more you care.' "

She heard shoes clacking on the tile, but connected the sounds with the approaching man only when he loomed over her. She began levering herself up from the couch, cringing and struggling in the cushions until finally Lee supported her elbow. Her head swam in dizziness, and she worried she'd already exposed some vulnerability, forfeited an advantage. When she recovered, she flashed Lee and the man a smile. Their eyes were waiting for her to fall.

She said, "Haven't keeled over yet."

Lee adjusted his sleeves; the man chuckled politely. In a voice like a doctor's, he said, "Mrs. Marshall, I'm Rudy Guerrero."

At first, she liked him calling her Mrs. Marshall, but walking to his office, she suspected the formality was a tactic to flatter widows, a calculated plea to trust his wet eyes and dark, expensive suit. She steeled herself. A large mahogany desk crowded the room, and she caught Lee admiring it. The Windberg painting on the wall was the same as the one in her oncologist's office, but she still liked it very much: a deer drinking from a creek, gauzy morning light shafting through vines. She was staring at the painting when Guerrero unbuttoned his jacket and sat in the deep leather chair. He opened an embossed folder, patted a handkerchief to his brow.

"Does a person absolutely have to be embalmed?" she asked.

Guerrero folded his hands together, glanced at Lee. "Well," he said, chuckling again. "State law doesn't require—"

"Perfect. Let's skip that."

Lee sighed. Guerrero twisted the ballpoint of a heavy silver pen into place. Nodding, he said, "A tough customer—I like it." Minnie heard the pen skimming across the desk. She glanced at Lee but he averted his eyes. Somehow she'd expected him to be pleased.

She arranged to draft monthly payments from her checking account; then, if necessary, her life insurance would cover the rest. More than anything, she wanted to pay off the funeral. She and Richard had never discussed this, but there seemed a tacit agreement that whoever lived longer would sacrifice for Lee. Her last duty was to be thrifty with her dying. The practicality buoyed her. But as she deliberated between grave vaults and cement casing, between a church funeral and a graveside service, Lee voted against her. She wanted a plaque where he wanted a monument. He cracked his knuckles and shifted in his seat. She suggested compromises when she could, but nothing satisfied him. Maybe a mother's funeral could never satisfy her son.

Then, so swiftly that she worried he'd overlooked something, Guerrero closed his folder and ushered them from his office. In the hall, she tried to touch Lee's cheek—a gesture to say, *We're doing fine, Good job, It's almost over*—but lifting her arm nearly toppled her and he had to grab her waist.

Guerrero opened a door past the floral displays and stepped demurely aside. He said, "I'll check back shortly."

The chilled air smelled of oak and lilacs, and it nearly buckled her knees. She felt dizzy, tasted bile in her throat; her stomach dropped. Three coffins—two open, one closed—rested on pedestals in the middle of the room. Sections of others, their hulls and sides, were affixed to the walls and illuminated by individual brass lamps. She had spent an afternoon in the showroom when Richard died but had insisted that Lee stay home. Now, he looked stunned, lost. She turned away to gather herself, feeling as though they'd happened upon a car accident. She imagined sitting beside the pond, heard herself telling Lee, "At least that's behind us." If they could only survive this, if she could hold it together, she thought Lee would reward her among the mesquite trees that hemmed the water; she plied herself with ideas of him shedding his layers of silence and talking with her in the sun.

She got her legs back slowly; the vertigo subsided. She made her way around the displays, fighting off the fearful reverence the room demanded. The poplar and maple and tucked satin seemed such a waste. The champagne-colored velvet and taffeta interiors were expensive and worthless. And the pillows! She'd forgotten coffins came with those. Who needed a pillow? Her heels clicked on the floor, like hammering in a church. When she moved into the steel displays—20-gauge, 18-gauge, stainless, what did it all mean? What did it matter?—she saw herself reflected in the gleaming surfaces. She winked at Lee in her reflection, but his eyes darted away.

She touched the firm, stitched padding; he clasped his hands behind his back.

"Now it feels like we *are* at a museum," she said. "We take a step and stop, then step and stop."

"A regular Smithsonian."

She laughed, though he gave her a cross look, and she realized he'd not meant to amuse her at all.

"Did I tell you what the French call guillotines?"

He nodded, inching back toward the oaks.

"The guillotines turned wives into widows," she said. He leaned to study a cherrywood casket. She said, "I like this one. It looks comfortable."

Basic steel, the shade of blush. Small gardenias, the same cream color as the satin lining, trimming the lid. A thin chrome bar along its side. She couldn't have cared less for it.

Lee said, "It's the cheapest."

"And the prettiest."

"What about this one? You love oak."

"Oh, it's beautiful, but you could fit three of me in there." She wanted him to laugh or at least smile—*please, please*—but he just paced forward, arms still behind his back. She said, "You look like a security guard."

Maybe she'd glimpsed a small grin forming, but if she had he'd squelched it and slid his hands into his pockets. If he'd been a child, she could have aped silly faces or ripped rags to cheer him, but now he was gone.

"Daddy's poodle used to bark at waves. At the beach, we'd—"

"The price doesn't matter, Mama."

"I know, honey. I just love this one, really. The gardenias are precious."

"You bought Dad a nice one."

She almost blurted, *He deserved a nice one,* but refrained. She crossed the room and pretended to consider the more expensive caskets. Lee said nothing. He'd turned callous and unreachable. She tried to remember which model she'd bought Richard, but couldn't. It had brass bars like saloon banisters, but none with bars looked familiar. Maybe the style was discontinued, but she felt certain the failing was hers. If she ruined everything else, shouldn't a widow at least remember her husband's casket? So much about her would disappoint him, her fear and depression, the burden she'd become for Lee, and the slow, sorry withering that now defined her life. Perhaps she was getting exactly what she deserved.

"Hello?" Guerrero stepped inside, hesitantly. "How are we?"

Minnie looked at Lee, then back at the man.

"Never better," she said. "I'll take this one."

LEE WANTED TO REST BEFORE THEIR PICNIC. HER choices had disheartened him, and though Minnie thought it better to eat lunch and get their minds off everything, she conceded. At home he retired to his room and left her to stew. Maybe he wanted to spare her his anger, but his silence was more punishing. And more exhausting. She had meant only to relax briefly, then start doing laundry, but in the recliner, the waking world receded. A patchwork of images—Guerrero's meaty hands and the painting behind his desk; Lee dropping her at various entrances to save her energy, then parking the car alone; Richard at the beach, holding a conch, saying *Hey, would you look at this*; a cakewalk from her youth, the music stopping precisely when she stepped onto the winning star—then she slept. In her dream, Richard appeared as a stranger, but she nonetheless recognized him as the man whose absence gripped her heart, and his voice poured like water. When she woke, the windows were black.

"Someone was tired," Lee said.

The raw light in the kitchen burned her eyes. She pulled a chair out from the table, and the legs scraping across the tile rankled her. Her lighter would not fire. She tried for what seemed minutes, then just as she resigned herself to getting a light from the stove, smoke filled her lungs. She exhaled with her eyes closed. Her mouth tasted clammy, sour. Lee was leering at her, she felt him. She hung the cigarette on her lips and went to the refrigerator for a Coke. He smiled as she crossed the kitchen, but she concentrated on not stumbling. Her head was clouded, her body more drained than before, sapped specifically of patience.

She held the bottle toward him. "I can't open this."

He twisted the cap, and the ease of the action seemed accusatory. In the garage, the washing machine buzzer sounded. She winced.

"Headache?" he asked.

"We missed the ducks."

"Maybe tomorrow. Maybe you'll feel better."

"I felt fine today," she said. "Besides, I have things to do tomorrow."

She half hoped he would call her bluff and argue (an unfamiliar yet powerful feeling), but he just went to move the laundry. Her legs were restless, small spasms jerking and knotting in her calves. Her stomach ached from not eating. All of her nerves felt exposed, stung by the light and air.

"Why didn't you wake me?" she asked when he returned. "I wanted to talk over lunch."

"We'll have a nice supper. We can talk now."

She dragged on her cigarette and stabbed the butt in the ashtray. In the window, her reflection appeared more diminished than it had even that morning.

"You just didn't want to go," she said, trying to light another cigarette.

"You needed rest." His tone was stoic and confident, meaning he thought he was right. Before, such willfulness had always comforted her; tonight it grated. He said, "How does cream of chicken sound?"

"What would have been so terrible about a picnic? The money? How much would we have spent? Twenty dollars? Can't we afford that on a day like today?"

"I'm not the one so concerned with money."

"A bronze grave vault is a bit excessive, Leiland."

He pinched the bridge of his nose, shut his eyes. "Is this the kind of night we're going to have?"

Maybe, she thought. She felt destitute of courtesy and tact, suddenly unconcerned with doing the right thing. Nothing had panned out as she'd wanted—nothing. She'd pinned her hopes on talking beside the pond, believing it would restore them, but now everything was dashed. She wanted to strike out, to be cruel, and nothing was worse than feeling this way toward him. Usually when he wanted to argue, she yielded. Yet before she knew she would say it, when she only knew she felt compelled to say something, she heard her voice: "I want to be cremated."

He put his hands on the window frame and gazed into the backyard. Or maybe his eyes were closed, maybe he was taking deep breaths, counting to ten. He said, "You need a nerve pill."

"No, Lee, I don't. You can't just dope me up all the time."

"Me? *Me* dope you up?"

"I can't talk to you. I can't even talk to my own son."

"What, Mother? What do you want to say?"

What did she want to say? Suddenly, nothing. Before, there seemed so much, but now everything had vanished. She said, "Sell the house, don't rent it."

"Oh, Jesus," he said—something she'd never heard him say.

"Sell the car. Take my jewelry to a jeweler. Not a pawnshop."

"Mother."

"Donate my wigs and clothes. That's what I want."

"Mother."

"I don't want you to be sappy. I want you to invest the money. If I want to be cremated, that's my choice. And if I want to have a picnic at the goddamned pond, the least—"

"Mother!" His voice rattled the windows, filled the room. Then silence filled it. When he spoke again, his tone had softened, as if in apology: "The pond is gone."

She shook out another cigarette. Her fingers trembled. "That's absurd."

"It's been gone for two years, maybe three. It's a car wash now. You sent me the newspaper clipping."

She shrugged. She flicked her lighter, and shook it, but it wouldn't catch. She tried and tried but got nowhere. She tossed the cigarette and lighter onto the table and held her face in her hands. Lee sulked into the hall. Her throat tightened; wet pressure welled behind her eyes. Hadn't they gone to the pond during chemo? She understood none of it, neither her son nor herself, their silences nor their arguments. She no longer knew his role or hers, what was required of her and what would handle itself; she didn't understand how to die. Lee ran water in the bathroom. She wanted to chase after him, to scream for help or ring her bell. She wanted to beg him not to shut himself in his room, wanted to dispense with the lie that today, or any day in the last year, was normal. Before, the charade seemed necessary for him, but now she realized she had depended upon it more than he ever had. He would survive this, rebuild a life that she would never see; a life, simply, without her. And shouldn't this please rather than terrify and anger her? She wanted to admit she was terrified, terrified to sleep or be awake, and she wished she'd lived a life different in every way except for him and his father; she wished she still had a chance. She wished she could bear to buy a beautiful coffin. She wished Richard were still alive, so Lee wouldn't have to drive her to the funeral home and watch her come undone. She wished, for all of their sakes, that she had died first.

He returned to the kitchen and said, "Just wait a minute. I'm going to the store."

She was trying the dead lighter again. He patted his pockets for his keys and wallet. She hated him driving to the store, because undoubtedly he thought if she didn't need lighters and cigarettes, she wouldn't be dying. He resembled his father, his thin hair and sloped shoulders and even his reticence, and as he checked the cupboards, the likeness was too much. All of it was too, too much. As the tears came, she wondered what else she'd forgotten or would forget, what else he was withholding. She wondered where the ducks had flown after the pond was gone, if he remembered how much he'd enjoyed them as a child. She wondered if he would ever have children, who would be their mother and what they would know of their grandmother. She wondered if they would get any of her features. The only trait that seemed worth passing on was her new lovely hair, which, really, wasn't hers at all.

IN A MONTH THE DEN WOULD BECOME A SICKROOM. A hospital bed would be delivered, tubes from the oxygen machine would snake over and behind her furniture; her furniture would be buried under hospice charts, hospital gowns, and packages of diapers. Nurses came and went. She held guarded conversations with them—as she had with Rudy Guerrero—but soon pockets of forgotten information devoured her speech. She would forget Lee's name. Though never who he was. Through that long, excruciating fade there always remained a silky, durable cord of memory that connected them, a child and his mother.

SHE WOKE IN THE RECLINER WITH THE TELEVISION on and Lee reading on the couch. Her mouth tasted dry. A new lighter, a pack of cigarettes and a chocolate bar lay beside the bell on the end table. She did not remember Lee settling her down or helping her into the recliner before going to the store. She remembered the fighting, and hoped it was over.

She said, "Good morning, sunshine."

He leaned forward, smiling in the lamplight. "It's almost midnight. I'll warm your soup."

She smoked as her eyes adjusted. Her body felt less fragmented, her thoughts less scattered. She was satisfied with the funeral arrangements and relieved to have them behind her. *A tough customer,* Guerrero had called her. After a few minutes, it occurred to her that she felt marvelous.

Lee returned with juice and soup and her nighttime medication, eight pills she had to swallow two at a time. He kissed her forehead, a gesture she adored but never admitted she adored for fear he would stop. He lay on the couch and hooked his arm over his eyes, crossed his ankles. As she ate—when had he learned to make such delicious soup, soup so good it made her hungrier to eat?—she noticed he wore socks she'd bought from a catalog. Sometimes just seeing him mystified her. Every night, he stayed awake long enough to make sure she wouldn't get sick. Every night she dreaded the moment he went to bed.

She relit her cigarette, drank more juice. She said, "Are you awake?"

"Okay," he said, startled. He raised his head, then lay back. "Yes, I am."

"Do you know what the French call—"

"The widow." He lifted his arm from his eyes and winked at her, smirking. Briefly she felt ashamed for repeating it— how many times had she told him?—then she let herself off the hook, because he had.

She said, "You're right about the pond."

He nodded, his elbow over his eyes again.

"And I don't want to be cremated."

"I know."

Four pills still waited beside the ashtray, though she recognized none of them. Lately, she remembered only the shapes of her muscle relaxers and nerve pills, the tablets she reached for most often. They bathed her in a perfectly warm, perfectly weightless oblivion, and as she melted, she wondered if the cottony nothingness enveloping her was how it would finally feel. She hoped so. In her darkest moods, she'd considered emptying the bottles and chasing the pills with vodka, but that would cancel her insurance. If Lee had to act as her nurse, she could at least pay for his trouble.

"Let's see if the ocean's still there," he said, suddenly.

She flinched. She'd thought he'd drifted to sleep. Then she heard the words as if in an echo, and her heart lurched.

"Dad used to come in my room and say that. I remembered it today."

Her skin tingled. How many times had she heard Richard say that, either to her or to Lee? The words lifted her, sent her memory reeling, as if in a second's time she'd gotten delightfully drunk.

"You'd still be in bed," he said. "We rarely went to the water, though. Usually he'd find some road to get lost on."

"Sounds familiar," she said. Maybe it sounded familiar, maybe not.

"So we were probably lost, but one morning he showed me where he'd buried Peppy."

She drew on her cigarette. A wave swelled beneath her. The tingling on her skin was replaced with a trembling in each nerve, an expectant hush.

"He said he'd convinced the vet to let him do it."

"What a thing to remember."

He uncrossed his ankles, then crossed them again. "I'd never seen him cry before. I must have been six or seven. I didn't know what to do."

She cleared her throat, quietly. "And?"

"I just waited," he said. "Eventually he quieted down and started the truck."

He was lying, of course, just as he had to explain the splotches in her peripheral vision, her illegible signature. Or he was exaggerating, suddenly committed to calming her. Perhaps now he couldn't ignore what was imminent, inevitable. Perhaps because she could no longer keep anything from him, he longed to resurrect and recast what he could for her. Probably he'd contrived his father's tears that afternoon or as she slept, but maybe he'd not imagined them until now. And what was he saying? That he was sorry? Or that he too would weep privately but eventually, begrudgingly, recover? None of it mattered; he was exalting her, filling her every cell with breath. She listened as she would to an opera, hearing not language but just his voice and its lament of time and love and doomed hopefulness. Oh, the surprise and absolute mystery of a child!

He said, "We'd go all over, those Saturday mornings."

It was as if he'd just returned from a long absence, or was a skittish animal finally coaxed into approaching. She turned to him, slowly, careful not to scare him away.

"Tell me," she said, putting out her cigarette. "Tell me where you've been."

Two Liars

WHAT I WANT TO EXPLAIN IS HOW MY FATHER became scared—desperate, really—and set fire to our house and cheated the insurance company out of its money. All of this happened in 1979. We lived on Whistler Road in Portland, Texas, a small town compared to Corpus Christi, but sizable when you included those living on the Naval Air Station, where my father worked. He left for his job hours before the morning paper came, so when he returned in the afternoons he read it, while chewing a thin cigar. Over the years, my mother has suggested that something he'd read triggered him, but I've never learned where all of our money had gone or what convinced my father we were in such poor shape. I was fifteen then and our lives seemed normal to me.

Robert Jackson—my father—was a man who knew how to do many things. The year I turned ten he added a second story to our house and only twice asked Obie Meek, our closest neighbor, for help. A year later, after a dainty-looking woman repossessed our new Datsun, he paid fifty dollars cash for a van with a fold-out bed, then rebuilt its engine to drive our family twelve hours for a vacation in Louisiana, the state of his birth. Both he and my mother kept pictures from that trip at work, hers in a gilded frame and his under a heavy sheet of glass on his desk. My father supervised the air-conditioning department at the base, and my mother worked as a secretary at a hardware company, where she sometimes stuffed new doorknobs and brass hinges into her purse. On weekends, my father installed them and I kneeled behind him, handing him tools.

The bad times started four years after he restored the van. It was early January, and I was working barefoot and barechested clearing dead limbs under our persimmon tree—there are no winters that far south. My parents sat inside wearing bifocals—though they were younger than most people who wear them—and punched our debts into an old calculator. I'd been sitting with them, but my mother asked me to water her garden after my father cracked his neck and started cursing about mortgages. Bad language was not uncommon around our house, so I didn't understand why my mother insisted that I leave, but I walked out the back door and toward her garden. When I passed the kitchen window and peeked at my parents, I saw their elbows on the table, their hands in the air. The window was raised, and as my father pushed back his chair and removed his glasses, he said, "We have to do *something*."

I thought he had suggested moonlighting to pay our bills—he'd done that in the past. Every couple of years he took jobs at a local garage, a furniture refinisher or a lumber-yard, and twice he worked as a night janitor at my school. Some mornings I opened my locker and found it cleaned and organized. Other times notes saying "Always look out for number one," or "Keep control, keep ahead," appeared in my desk. They were written in my father's small, stiff print on yellow squares of paper, which I crumpled before messing up my locker. I told people that the school had contracted him to do air-conditioning work. It usually took the same amount of time for my father to exhaust himself with two jobs that it did for him to grow comfortable with our finances again, and eventually, each time, my mother would convince him to quit.

On that January evening, he marched into the yard and touched my shoulder. He told me to go back inside and help my mother wash the dishes, then he disappeared into the garage. My mother closed the window when I stepped inside.

"We're in a scrape now, Toby," she said, her hands invisible in the gray water filling the sink. "Your father feels boxed in."

I stood beside her and toweled the dishes she handed me. "Is he going to find another job?"

"No." She blew a few strands of hair from her face. "I don't know what's going to happen."

"I bet we'll end up fine," I said, and at that time I believed it. But my mother understood that we were living with a man who wanted another life for us.

She scrubbed the remaining dishes and handed them to me in silence. Then she dried her hands. "People go crazy at

times," she said. "They think in ways you can't understand."
She was talking about my father, and when I saw him later
that night I wondered what he'd done to make her say that.
He was scanning the want ads and didn't look insane. I didn't
disturb him, but went to the window and looked at the yard,
perfectly trimmed.

I was earning fine grades. Aside from Olaf Hollins, a kid in
my class who'd promised to punish me for refusing to write a
paper for him, school never troubled me because I had a good
memory and liked reading. My father tacked my report cards
to a corkboard above his desk and told everyone I would go to
medical school. Neither of my parents had graduated the
eighth grade, so they pampered me when it came to my studies.
But I wanted something else. I wanted to listen to a car's engine
and understand why it stalled. I wanted to know the difference
between a catalytic converter and a driveshaft, the ability to
distinguish a burned-out clutch from a shot transmission by the
odor. These were my father's talents, things he mentioned in
conversations like names of relatives. But he denied them to
me, deeming me too intelligent to clutter my mind with such information. "You'll have a different life than me," he'd said
more than once. "When you need something fixed, you'll hire
someone." These words came from beneath one of our vehicles, and in between them my father described what I should
hand him. Every time I placed a tool into his greasy palm, I
memorized its name, hoping he would quiz me on it later.

But I believed that my father's refusal to teach me about
his tools stemmed from something I'd done wrong. Maybe I'd

answered a question in a way he didn't appreciate, or maybe he never forgot that in grade school a girl had blackened my eye. Or maybe it hadn't happened yet. Maybe he saw something in me, a potential for a flaw in my character, that discouraged him. Maybe he knew that in a crunch, I would hesitate and flounder, or I would rush and cut the wrong wire.

"I'm sorry," I said when I crossthreaded a nut on my bicycle—when I busted his shovel, when I swallowed a mouthful of gasoline while learning to siphon, when I knocked a hole in a piece of Sheetrock.

"It's not your fault." His voice would be calm, his mind already assessing the damage, plotting the repair. "It was my mistake."

"I'll do it right the next time."

"No, Toby." He always used my name when he tried to console me. My father was good at consoling people. "We're done with that now," he'd say and change the subject, and no matter how I tried to pull the conversation back, I would fail. The blame was his now, and it too was out of my range. He'd carry it with him, and I would follow, waiting for another chance to feel close to him. But he would never relinquish it. It would stay with him for the rest of his life, and even after he died any sense of complicity would evade me. I would try to find it, to seize that quality of my father's which was lost on me, but my attempts were always anchored in inability, as if I lacked the right tools, as if my small, clumsy hands were trying to grab smoke.

———

THE PREVIOUS CHRISTMAS, MY PARENTS HAD DE-cided not to exchange gifts. I'd overheard them agreeing on this but didn't believe it until I actually saw that the only presents they got were what my grandmother and I had given them. They unwrapped a wallet and set of stationery from me, and sweat suits from my grandmother, black for him, pink for her. But neither handed a gift to the other. It still seemed like a good time in our lives, and I hoped that in the future we would look back on it and smile. We were sitting on the floor and listening to my grandmother's holiday records, when, as my mother pushed herself up from the carpet, my father asked, "Is that a bird in the tree?"

It was absurd, yes, but we all turned toward the Christmas tree, and on his urging, my mother spread the limbs to look for the bird. "Stop teasing," she said, and though it sounded like she was going to say my father's name, her mouth opened too wide for words when her eyes lit on the thin gold chain hanging among the tinsel. She hesitated before taking it from the branches, and when she turned—eyes fixed on the necklace, tinsel tangled in her hair—she only shook her head. Nothing would have pleased her more than to have given my father one small gift, while nothing would have made him more angry, and even then I knew that. When my mother started crying, my father rose and held her to him. He smirked and accused her of scaring away the bird. Then they didn't say anything for some time.

After the new year, they started working more overtime and spoke of selling my mother's car. I said I could find a job—Portland is a town where a boy of fifteen can find dock work and get paid in cash—but my father insisted that I concentrate on school. We canceled our newspaper delivery, and my father pawned his rifle and some of my mother's rings. Every night my parents suggested ideas to each other, things they'd fretted over all day. Then they argued. Once I overheard my mother say she would not be a party to such a thing, and if he tried to drag her son down with him, she would disappear with me. That fight ended like the others: My father withdrew into the garage while my mother walked around our block. I closed myself in my room, as if hiding from a tornado, waiting for it to tear the tar-paper roof off our home.

"THE ONLY IRREPLACEABLE THING IS FAMILY," MY father said as he and I drove to straighten my grandmother's garage. My mother was already there.

At first I let the words pass over me. In my mind I questioned whether he'd even said anything at all. I could only guess that he was laying the groundwork to confide to me that my grandmother was dying, which she was, but we never spoke of it.

"This van, our house, jewelry, money—they all come and go." He shifted gears and went silent.

"I know."

"I'm not a rich man and I'm not smart, but I'd do anything for my family. I would do anything for you."

"I think you're smart," I said, and it was true.

"I'm not. I've got good sense, but I'm not smart." He didn't look at me. "You're smart."

"I'd do anything for my family, too. I'd do anything for you."

"Don't ever get sentimental, boy. Ever."

We pulled into the driveway leading to my grandmother's small house, gravel snapping against the van's carriage. I thought we'd knock on her door and drink a glass of iced tea before beginning, but without telling anyone we'd arrived, my father and I went straight to work. When the sun started to drop, my grandmother eased herself down the steps and into the garage. The smell of lilacs followed her and she patted my wrist when she stepped close to me. My mother stayed in the house, watching us from the doorway. She looked tired. "Oh, yes," my grandmother said, seeing all the space we'd cleared. "I told her there'd be plenty of room, probably some to spare."

That night, Obie came over and my father invited him to stay for dinner. He and my parents drank some beer after we ate, though by nine o'clock my mother had gone to bed and left the three of us watching television. My father poked into their room after a minute, and I thought he would just kiss her good night and return soon, but he stayed in there. Obie scanned the channels and said, "Your parents really love you."

I didn't know how to respond. "Thank you," I said.

"All day at work your old man raves about you." He crushed an empty pack of cigarettes and dropped it into his lap. Obie's wife had left him two years before, and he told prison stories, though we knew he'd only spent two nights in the county jail for unpaid tickets. "Did he tell you about that rattlesnake?"

I said he didn't.

"Some old boy from the base set one loose in another old boy's truck. Can you believe that?" Obie shook his bald head. Then, maybe because he was telling the story, I pictured a snake slithering inside the trashed Dodge Charger Obie kept on cinder blocks in his driveway.

"Yes. I believe that."

"Then that second old boy put a trash can full of rotten shrimp on the other's porch, and set it on fire." Obie scratched his pink scalp. "I'm sure your dad will tell you. Just act surprised."

My father stepped out of the bedroom then, and for some reason I thought my mother was still awake and thinking about us. His eyes appeared hard at that moment, focused on something I couldn't see, though he quickly snapped back to himself.

Soon Obie left, and I considered asking my father about the snake, but finally didn't. We stayed up past the hour when all the stations except PBS sign off. A program about a man missing one leg came on, and we learned that he'd been trapped under a rock while hiking in Yellowstone Park. The man—the program labeled him "Joseph Henson, Survivor"—freed himself except for his right ankle, which remained hopelessly lodged. He claimed to have heard wolves howling in the woods and had seen bear tracks not fifty yards from where he lay helpless. But what finally drove him to rip off his sleeve, tourniquet his calf, and saw off his leg with a pocketknife was the cold. "No one was going to save me," Joseph Henson said. "I was either going to freeze to death or hack off my foot." He dragged himself to a ranger station and lost everything from his knee down, due to complications. The camera panned across his family and dropped to his plastic leg. He explained that when he detached the prosthetic he could still feel the ghost of his real limb and sometimes reached to scratch it. My father and I sat in awe, watching Joseph Henson as intently as we would've watched a live broadcast of the Resurrection.

"What else was he going to do?" my father said and took a swallow of beer. "Desperate son of a bitch."

ON THE LAST SUNDAY IN JANUARY MY PARENTS again sat at the kitchen table, plugging away at the calculator. I studied beside them. My homework lay scattered among their ledgers, receipts, bills, insurance papers.

"Done," my father said. He removed his glasses and rubbed his dark eyelids. "They're all paid."

I looked at him, less because of what he said than the way he said it. His words sounded stiff, rehearsed.

"Why don't we just pay a couple a month?" My mother seemed to be thinking aloud. "If you want to know what I'd like, that's what it would be. To take our time about this."

"We're fine this way."

"How much is left?" she asked.

My father shook his head to mean he didn't want to answer her. "Jean."

"What about college?" She darted her eyes at me.

"Jean."

"We can't afford this." My mother touched her fingers to her lips and held them there for a few seconds.

"They're *almost* paid now. Is that better?" He rolled his shoulders. "We're in good shape."

"You have no idea what you're doing."

My mother wanted to say more. I heard that in the silence. But she only stared at my father; his hands hid his eyes. They stayed like that for what seemed like a long time, then she grabbed her cigarettes and barged outside into the night. My father exhaled, loudly, then started double-checking his calculations. After every ten or twelve keystrokes, he raised his eyes over his glasses to consult his figures. He appeared to know what he was doing. The only thing that made him look like a man who wasn't an accountant was the scar splitting his left eyebrow.

"How did you get your scar?" I knew the story but wanted to hear him tell me again. At that moment I wanted to hear my father's voice.

A man had hit him. My parents had stopped for gas in Baton Rouge, and the man shouted obscenities at my mother as she walked to the restroom. As my father spoke, he didn't look at me, so I tried to see my mother outside, but I only saw the two of us reflected in the windows. My father had ignored the man in Baton Rouge until he ran toward my mother. He said he'd forgotten how he'd been hit, that he hadn't even noticed until they were back on the road, which seemed impossible to me.

"What about the man?"

"I clocked him with a tire iron and left him on the cement." My father looked at me for the first time. "Your mother had nightmares about him, but she's forgotten him now. Every so often I wonder about him, but it doesn't matter. Maybe he died right there."

My father returned to his numbers then, and I imagined telling him I'd hit Olaf Hollins with a tire iron. Olaf muscled everyone around at my school. He took mostly shop classes and smoked while he worked. His shelves and footstools earned A's, while mine always wobbled and splintered. But I thought of hitting Olaf because he knew that he terrified me, and I didn't want my father to know anything scared his son.

IN THE WEEK AFTER MY FATHER SAID HE'D PAID our bills, we ate at restaurants with cloth napkins and my mother received roses at work. My parents went out alone on the first Friday in February and left me twenty dollars for pizza; I stashed it in the jar that I kept under my bed—a sign of thrift I'd always believed would please my father—and watched a baseball game until they returned. My mother came in first, and only huffed the word "Unbelievable," then dropped her purse onto the floor, where it fell over. I could hear her keys and compact topple onto the wood. A minute later my father entered, closed the door behind him, and gathered the contents of the purse. Crouching there, he said to me, "Get some sleep. Tomorrow we're painting the house."

We started before dawn, me stirring the paint and my father taping our windows and bunching tarps around the foundation. I wanted to ask questions, but we spoke very little. It was difficult to see my hands or what color paint I was mixing, and twice I tripped and fell to the hard, black ground. My father showed me how to brush in long vertical strokes, though after I botched a section that he would have to sand and repaint, he relegated me to cleaning our work area.

Around noon my mother stepped outside and loaded a box into her car. It occurred to me that she might be leaving and might take me with her, but when I asked my father what she was doing, he said she was taking things to my grandmother's. When she appeared again, handling another, smaller box, I asked her why she wasn't helping. I intended it as a joke.

"This is your father's project." She sounded irritated and shot a look at him. He was rinsing his brush with gasoline.

"You'll like it when it's done," he said.

Then she ducked into the car, started it and drove away.

Each afternoon we painted for two hours when my father returned from the base. I felt good helping him, so good that I thought about little else. My technique improved and mostly he stopped inspecting my work. When we began preparing to paint the interior, we started sleeping at my grandmother's to escape the fumes. My father asked Obie to watch the house in the evenings and handed him a piece of paper with my grandmother's phone number on it. He commented on how fine the paint looked, but also ribbed my father about how long the job was taking. A couple of times Obie invited him to take a break and drink a beer with him, which he did, then he returned and worked meticulously as a thief.

When we started making progress, my father suggested I invite some friends over to show off our work. I decided against this because it seemed a strange thing to do, but a few of my parents' friends visited and offered compliments. Each day my father and I inched our ladders and buckets farther around our house. Inside, my mother dusted and rearranged with the windows open. She would poke her head out and ask where my father put their wedding album or where I kept my old scout uniform. She packed these things to store in my grandmother's garage while my father and I sanded small sections of our house, working until it grew too dark to see.

My grandmother's house was close to the beach and had two bedrooms. She slept in hers, my parents took the guest room, and I spent nights on the tweed couch that itched my skin. Soon I started sleeping in the van. I snuck out after everyone retired for the night and shambled inside with the sunrise, well before my father started frying eggs for breakfast. Ever since we'd started sleeping there, my parents fought more. My mother didn't like for my grandmother to hear them, so they yelled behind the guest room door and ignored each other at dinner, passing helpings without allowing their eyes to meet.

On the night that everything happened, my father stepped out of his room wearing the black sweat suit my grandmother had given him for Christmas, which made her smile. It was the first time I'd seen him since the morning; he'd worked on the house without me that afternoon. I'd come home, ready to paint, but he'd left a note telling me to take the day off because I'd been doing such a fine job. That evening, he didn't say anything to me or my grandmother but excused himself to go outside. The smell of sweet cigar smoke crawled under the door. A few minutes later my mother stepped into the hallway and stood still, as if she were lost and confused about where to go. Then she moped into the den and lay on the couch, resting her head in my grandmother's lap. Seeing her like that saddened me. We watched the late newscast, but in the middle of it she raised herself from the couch and clicked it off. "I would like to hear happy stories sometimes," she said and walked down the hall. "I would like to hear that things are improving."

That night I decided against pulling out the bed but just stretched out on the van's couch and thought about my mother. I fell asleep still in my clothes, trying to remember a positive news story and could only think of Joseph Henson's, one she did not know.

I AWOKE SHORTLY AFTER HE CRANKED THE ENGINE. Outside the night was a dark, dark blue and I lay as still as I could, wondering what I should do, where he was going. The van was cruising slowly and my father turned off the radio. In the driver's seat he mouthed something, and though I couldn't decipher his words I thought he was making a list. And just as I resigned myself to staying hidden and waiting to see what would happen, the van stopped and his eyes fixed me in the rearview mirror. They narrowed in a way that made me cold. He glared at me, but I turned to the window and realized we were parked near our house. We stayed quiet. He was quiet, I think, because he felt trapped and didn't know how to proceed, and I was quiet because I could think of nothing to say.

"I was asleep," I said.

He continued staring at me in an awful way, as if I'd accused him of having an affair, which was something that had crossed my mind. His eyes held me for several long seconds before he said, "Get out of the van." All I could think was that we were going to paint. My father eased the door closed behind me, to the point where it rested on its casing and the interior light dimmed. We crept to our porch. Clouds covered the small moon and no porch lamps burned on Whistler Road. We moved in darkness, me behind my father. When I asked again what we were doing, he raised his hand for me to hush, so I did. I fell in behind him and in front of me he became invisible.

Inside, we turned on no lights. My father hustled around the house picking up things and replacing them, as if he'd lost something. The air reeked of turpentine. He whispered that we wouldn't stay long and vanished into his bedroom. Because I could think of nothing else, I went into my room and looked it over without the lights. My eyes had adjusted to the darkness, but I still couldn't see clearly and stretched my arms out to keep from bumping into things. The squeaks of drawers opening and closing sounded behind me, and soon my father entered with a satchel over his shoulder. He handed it to me and my arm jerked with its weight, then he said to wait outside.

"Wait for what?"

"For me," he said, ferreting through the cupboards.

"I feel like we're robbing ourselves." I laughed a little and expected him to smile. But he only repeated for me to go outside. And though I never actually thought we were stealing what we already owned, I realized that whatever we were doing was something other fathers and sons did not do.

Sitting on our porch, I felt vulnerable, yet standing up made my hands seem heavy and awkward. Painting equipment lay around the foundation of our house, strewn in a way that my father had chided me for in the past. Even in the moonlight I could see paint drying in the bristles of brushes, and cans left open since that afternoon, two of them fallen over and bleeding onto the leaves of my mother's flower bed. I peeked inside to find my father, and when I didn't see him, I moved to clean up the mess. But before I took two steps I stopped, and inched back to our porch, where I glimpsed him inside. He patted his pockets, and the tip of his cigar glowed like lava. Everything fell silent. I turned away and he came outside and locked the door behind him. We drove away without turning on our lights.

———

MY GRANDMOTHER ANSWERED THE PHONE AND screamed, screamed in a way you do not want to hear anyone close to you scream. We sped to our house still wearing pajamas. My grandmother sobbed and I kept asking what had happened, but my parents never answered. The sun was just starting to climb through the morning clouds, but enough light filtered down to see the house was a complete loss. The fire was out, but its wet-tar odor lingered; flames smell different than smoke. My mother collapsed into my grandmother's arms, the way I pictured our second story collapsing onto our first. Obie dawdled around, adjusting his glasses and trying to comfort everyone by squeezing their shoulders. Everything was black and saturated and reeking of sulfur. I feared causing more damage, cringing every time a piece of wood or glass cracked beneath my feet. I tiptoed to where my room had been and tried to identify things. Water seeped into my shoes and soaked my socks. I remembered that pioneers had burned old barns to save the nails and I wondered what anyone could salvage from our house. The firemen talked and gestured to my father, circling our foundation. I heard two-by-fours snap beneath their feet, and they kicked pieces of our walls and rummaged through ashes of the attic. One of them asked my father if he had any enemies and he answered that he had no more than any man. Then they spoke of turpentine and electrical shorts.

My mother sifted through the remains of her garden. Charred paint cans cluttered the small space where she used to plant her bulbs. She stood and placed her palms on my cheeks and looked into my eyes as though she wanted to apologize for all of this. Her hands bruised my face with soot, and I felt myself start crying. She pulled me to her and over her shoulder I noticed the small plastic fence around her garden. Much of it had melted into nothing, but a few of the stakes had survived the blaze. They remained blackened and gnarled, bowed in on themselves, pointing at each other like fists.

FIRE INVESTIGATORS AND INSURANCE ADJUSTERS ruled that faulty wiring had caused the blaze. When my father relayed this news, it was the first time in two days that we'd heard his voice. My parents didn't speak much during this time—to each other or to me. And, like them, I held my tongue.

We stayed at my grandmother's. One night my mother stalked into the living room as I was trying to fall asleep. She smelled of salt water and cigarette smoke, a combination of scents that still conjures her image. She wore a dress I didn't recognize, but this might have been because very little light shafted through the blinds. I thought again that she was leaving, and it surprised me when she sat down in my grandmother's chair.

"I went for a walk on the beach," she said, as if answering a question.

I adjusted my pillow, doubled it over so I could see her better.

She exhaled. The sound made me expect a ribbon of blue smoke to stream from her mouth, but it didn't. "My father was a fisherman. Did you know that?"

"Yes."

"A shrimper," she said. "His boat was named *The Reina*."

I remembered the man and that his skin felt like an old football. I looked hard at my mother then, at her skin, and for the first time realized that she had once been beautiful.

"He told us stories." She pulled at the hem of her skirt, and then placed her hands in her lap, where they reminded me of baby birds. "I think I'm a poor mother because I can't remember any stories for you."

This, to me, was not why she felt like a poor mother, though I didn't say that.

"But I thought of something tonight. Something he used to say, and I want to tell it to you now."

I said okay, but a moment passed before she spoke.

"The ocean has no memory."

And although she stayed in the room with me, this was the last thing my mother said that night. Something outside, maybe a raft of clouds floating across the moon, eclipsed what light slanted inside, and the room fell to blackness. My father rolled over in the next room. When my mother stood, I thought she would go to him or maybe leave through the front door, but she took off her shoes, one then the other, and lowered herself onto the couch beside me. She wiggled into the blanket and became still. I draped my arm over her and her back relaxed into my chest. She seemed to fall asleep, but her body remained tense; under my arm, it felt like one strained muscle. Soon, though, the muscle released and she slipped into quiet, reluctant whimpers, then finally she began to really cry. I doubted her thoughts were far from mine.

WE MOVED INTO OUR NEW HOUSE IN THE MIDDLE of summer. A claims adjuster called daily and visited almost as often. Now I think his frequent visits meant that our family was under some suspicion, but at the time I only knew that my father preferred to talk to him alone and eventually the man ruled the reason the fire had spread so quickly was because of the turpentine and scattered painting supplies. Accelerants, he called them. Furniture came slowly, due to a delay with the insurance, so we slept in sleeping bags and ate on the floor like campers. The house was smaller than our other one, yet it seemed bigger, emptier, and though my father had installed a window air conditioner, the cloistering heat was stifling. The end of summer approached, and we probably looked like any other family getting used to their new house, except ours smelled like someone else's home. One night when we returned from buying groceries, my father's key broke off in the lock.

The last check cleared by the end of August, and we finished arranging the house before I returned to school. My mother started lifting alloy hinges and antique light-switch casings to replace the cheap ones in the house, and my father stained cabinets on weekends. The house evolved into something resembling our old one, if only in stolen fixtures and the smell of varnish. And also like before, my father refused to let me help with the renovations. We started eating homemade dinners, then retiring to the den and watching cable. On weekends we slept late, and during the week we moved through the house with a forced familiarity. With every new pillow or set of curtains, we grew more comfortable. A few times, Obie visited, and my parents started laughing again.

The night before school started my father drove me to the bay. He told my mother we were meeting Obie, and whether or not this was supposed to have been true, we never did. We went to the private piers in Corpus where doctors and lawyers docked their sailboats. Security lights illuminated the area and a guard paced in front of the yachts. Gulls squawked above us, though they only became visible when they swooped into the light; they looked like silver fish swimming through black water. We walked to the end of a pier and leaned against the guardrail, where my father opened his pocketknife and began shaving his fingernails. He cut toward his body, a way he'd cautioned me against, and let the edges of his nails spiral into the ocean. The waves walloped against the pylons, their foam like a lazy, iridescent serpent caught in low tide. My hands stayed in my pockets. "Where's Obie?"

"I guess he got tied up." My father looked into the sky.

The security light caught the blade of his knife, and I watched him slice into his thumbnail.

"He thinks someone from the base torched our house, Obie does. I wonder, Toby, what you think."

I shrugged and leaned over the guardrail, trying to watch one of my father's nails fall to the water. I thought of the story Obie had told me about the rattler and how the men who worked under my father resented him. Of course I didn't say any of that, though I don't think it would've angered my father.

"Obie's a good man," he said, and I looked at his face. My father bestowed this honor on very few, and I immediately admired anyone who received it. "He's smart."

"Sometimes I think Obie lies."

"He does. You're right." His voice was low; he was focusing on his hands.

"I try not to lie." I paused, waiting for him to commend me, but he didn't. "I don't think you lie."

"I have lied. But I would never lie to you. Or to your mother."

"I've lied—"

"You can ask me anything in the world and I'll tell you the truth as I know it." My father continued to stare at his fingers, so I looked as well, finding his blade taking dead skin with the nail. I thought hard for something to ask him, something to test his claim, but found nothing. He continued, "Sometimes there's a difference between telling the truth and telling everything."

My father looked at me then, harshly, and I remembered painting two and sometimes three coats over stubborn sections of our home. I also remembered his note saying I'd done a good job, but that he hadn't allowed me to work at the new house. I considered asking him about it, or if he'd really paid all our bills that night at the kitchen table. But I said, "You can ask me anything too."

He brushed the tips of his fingers against his palm, and from his knotted brow, I supposed he was trying to find something to ask me.

"I don't need to," he said, clipping his knife closed. "I know I can trust you. You're my son and we're in this together." He placed his hand on my shoulder and squeezed chills into my neck. His touch seemed to say that soon no secrets would wedge their way between us. We stood there for a few minutes, on the verge of truth and change, two liars staring down the darkness.

WE NEVER AGAIN SPOKE OF THE FIRE, DESPITE WHAT I hoped. Especially in the days after the night on the pier, the topic seemed to exist just beneath all our words, our movements, so that soon it would burst through the thin barrier between us. But it didn't. The days became weeks, and though I felt my father was only waiting for the right time to explain things to me, the chance of that happening was as slim then as it was a month later, when he died.

He was reshingling the roof. As the doctor explained it to my mother and me, sitting in a cramped room with only a sofa, an end table, and a small brass crucifix, his heart exploded. I knew he was dead, but I thought an exploding heart sounded nice, as if it were my father's kindness that had killed him. My mother sat beside the doctor, her hands covering her eyes. A priest knocked on the door, then entered. The room seemed very crowded. We listened as he said we could find comfort in my father's quick, painless passage to the eternal.

But almost before he finished his sentence, my mother wiped her eyes with the back of her hand and said, "I find no fucking comfort in my husband's death."

After my father's funeral, I hated going home. The house felt too spacious, and its emptiness constricted me. My mother took an extended leave from work to stay in her bedroom all day and sleep on the couch at night. I tore the posters off my walls and pushed my bed to the middle of my room. Even then I saw the pathetic nature of our attempts at recovery. One night I came home later than usual and found her asleep at the kitchen table. Her nightgown had fallen open and I could see the bottom of her neck where my father's wedding ring dangled from that thin gold chain. I couldn't help staring any more than I could move to wake her. I watched her chest fall and rise, and I flinched when the phone rang. My mother came briefly to life and answered, spoke for a few minutes, then handed me the receiver without a word. In my grandmother's voice I could hear the cancer that would kill her in less than a year.

When I returned to school, people touched me. Hands fluttered to my shoulders and arms pulled me toward bodies I didn't remember knowing. Teachers, students, janitors, almost everyone missed my father and apologized about his death. I thanked them and rushed to class before I started crying.

In the middle of a lunch period, as I dropped the food I hadn't eaten into the trash, a heavy hand pressed itself into the small of my back and a voice said, "I'm really sorry about your dad." When I turned, Olaf Hollins was nodding sympathetically.

"What?"

"Your father." He glanced over each of his shoulders. "I'm really sorry he passed away. I sold him some paint when I worked at McCoy's."

Just then, maybe because he seemed like the boy my father might've been, I punched Olaf Hollins in the throat. He gasped and his eyes widened like a shot deer's as he tumbled into the stack of trays, knocking them down and filling the cafeteria with the loud, sharp sound of trouble. He held his neck as if he were strangling himself and scuttled backward across the floor, like a crab, small and awkward and afraid. Everyone glared at me. Someone went for the principal, and as I waited for him I envisioned my fate: His office would feel cold and clean. He would look at my record and act kindly because of my grades and extenuating circumstances, and I would sit quietly when he said, "This is a tough time." I would not answer when he questioned my relationship with Olaf. Did I know him outside of school? Had there been static between us before? Was there anything he should know? Only when he asked how I felt would I say, "Fine."

Of course, I was lying. The truth? I woke up every morning forgetting that my father was dead and expected to hear him frying eggs in the kitchen. When reality knocked me down, I crawled back into bed and bawled like a girl. It became difficult for my mother and me to talk, and soon our grief embarrassed me enough to lie about my age and enlist in the Navy as my father had. Maybe the principal understood this, since he let me off with a warning. Maybe he knew how many times I replayed the memory of standing on the pier with my father. Maybe he knew that years later I would still smell the scent of my father on my clothes and sulfur in my hair, on my skin. Maybe, sitting across from me, he saw that I felt anything but fine, that I felt betrayed and alone, as if someone had set fire to my house and I was too far away to do anything but watch it burn.

Anything That Floats

"MY MOTHER DUMPED MY FATHER FOR AN ostrich farmer," Vince said yesterday. We were in a semiprivate room in the heart wing of Spohn Hospital. I lay on the other bed and said, "Did she now?" but just thought the codeine drip was scrambling his memory in lascivious ways. Today he's lucid again, eating and joking about his IV, and when our son, Tyler, starts in about wanting to go swimming, Vince looks at me and tells us to get lost.

So I'm driving to the Catalina Motel; our regular pool at the rec center is closed because the city's in a drought. This is an unseasonably mild afternoon in Corpus Christi because there's a trough of cool air in the Gulf. I try to see that patch of distant coolness, as if it were a cloud. Instead there is only the soapy, opaque bay, a few collapsed beach umbrellas in front of the condos, and the trees along the seawall whose dry, brown palms hang like scraps of parchment. Tyler sits cross-legged in the passenger seat. He's reading a book on boa constrictors—one, I believe, that he stole from the hospital library.

Our house is full of snakes. When we learned Tyler was allergic to pet dander and had to give our collie to a woman with acreage in Orange Grove, he and his father convinced me to let him keep a garter snake in his room. Now we have two gray rat snakes trying to mate in an aquarium under one of my old curtains, a banded king snake that eats only after dark, a corn snake and an albino bull snake under heat lamps in the garage, and a lazy royal python in a terrarium behind the kitchen table. Each week we buy seven mice (the python gets two) that Tyler drops into the cages. The owner of the pet store is smitten with him, with his unlikely and considerable knowledge; she arranged his job lecturing at the museum. On the third Saturday of every month, families and retiree tours pay to hear my eight-year-old son speak on the surprisingly docile temperament of death adders.

"This book is wrong," he says now. "It says retics are the biggest."

Retics are reticulated pythons; we did a book report. They're the second-largest snakes in the world, though now I can't recall the name of the longer one—possibly it's a boa. Ahead, the ceramic seahorse perched atop the motel becomes visible. I say, "Maybe they found a longer one."

"Doubtful," he says, never lifting his eyes.

On the awning above the U-shaped driveway, the word "Catalina" is scripted in elegant curlicues, but "Motel" is in block letters. This has always struck me as cheap and sexy, like blue eye shadow. Two cars are parked by Room 17, and the flatbed trailer with the broken window units is still behind the whirlpool gazebo. A sign on the hurricane fence around the pool reads: YE OLDE SWIMMIN' HOLE.

I say, "We're the only ones here. You can practice your dives."

"Where's the diving board?"

In the rearview mirror, my face is that of a woman who spent the night on a hospital cot. I say, "You can practice from the side."

In June, his father brought home the advertisement for the Anything-That-Floats-But-A-Boat event at this year's Bayfest, and he told Tyler that if by the end of the summer he could dive without belly flopping and tread water for three minutes, they would enter. Before two of Vince's ventricles seized shut and his boss from the shipyard called me to meet him at Spohn Hospital, the two of them—Vince and Tyler—spent evenings designing their vessel. The last drawing showed a plastic barrel housed in the middle of a plywood X. The sketches lie on the bedside table in the hospital, but he hasn't picked them up again. Bayfest starts in three weeks.

The Catalina will get busy tonight. Room doors are open and laundry carts are out. As always, Christmas lights dress the balcony eaves. Tyler stands on the edge of the deep end, wearing lizard-print trunks; most everything he wears depicts a reptile. He looks puzzled, concerned. He hasn't swum since Vince was admitted, and he's losing his tan. Still, his skin is almondy like his father's. Once, crossing the border back from a day in Mexico, Vince had to show his driver's license and answer various patriotic questions to prove residency. I was feeding Tyler in the passenger seat, expecting the officers to make my husband sing the "Star-Spangled Banner," when I realized I'd dreamt the ordeal years before.

"Maybe you should practice floating first," I say. "Maybe it's too shallow for good dives."

He nods, defeatedly, but he's relieved to have me to blame. Diving still scares him. He lowers his feet into the water, then drops in completely. While he's under, I glance toward the office, and Gilbert Salazar's already crossing the caliche parking lot. He's chewing a toothpick, watching the ground as he passes through the lattice gate. He scoots a cedar bench under its picnic table and walks the length of the pool to stand at the foot of my plastic lounge chair. Tyler breaches the surface, then ducks under again.

Gilbert says, "Ma'am, may I see your room key?"

Maybe he wants me to give him a thrill by flashing the key to Room 22, but I've not seen it in months. For a while I expected Vince to toss it like an accusation onto the kitchen table, but now I think it fell from my pocket in a Laundromat dryer. I admit the prospect of saying something coquettish *does* excite me—something like, "My husband has it"—but I don't want that hassle. I say, "I know the manager."

The toothpick jumps to the other side of his mouth. A breeze riffles the dried-up crape myrtle on the fence, and with the clouds dispersing, the sun casts a harsh ivory glow on the bricks around the pool; the water catches the light like a sapphire. Gilbert eyes the book on boas, says, "You like big snakes?"

"My son does." My answer comes so fast he probably thinks I've missed his point. Behind Gilbert, Tyler floats on his back, eyes closed.

"Certainly," Gilbert says. "The little snake king, the giver of speeches."

"If we're disturbing the guests, we can leave. Or I can pay—"

"Today, of all days, is when I wear a guayabera."

I smile, letting my eyes linger on the embroidered shirt, his trunks that are a size too small. This little show is why, of the many motel pools in Corpus, I've brought us here, for a reprieve from the hospital and transplant negotiations. I say, "I wondered what you'd be wearing."

"Do you know what I wonder? I wonder how long since Colleen's visited old Gil."

When I stay quiet, he pivots toward the pool. Tyler is spitting water like a fountain; he's trying to spray a sun-whitened NO LIFEGUARD sign.

It was short-lived, maybe two months, over a year ago. Gilbert had come into the showroom—I sell pool supplies—because the filter on the deep end was collecting algae. Vince had recently admitted about Annette Maldonado, so I told Gilbert I'd have to see the filter firsthand to diagnose the trouble. "Diagnose" was the word I used, and every time I hear it now, I recall the itchy seafoam bedspread in Room 22. Whether Vince knows about Gilbert is not something I've discerned. During the bypass surgery, one of my disgusting thoughts was that if he died, at least he'd never learn about Gilbert. There was mercy there, but also a repulsive, traitorous relief.

Tyler pushes himself out of the pool and comes slapping his feet on the polished aggregate, trailing shallow puddles that immediately evaporate. He pauses beside a rolling barbecue pit to shake water from his ears. I work his towel out from under me. He says, "I dreaded for four minutes, possibly five."

"*Treaded,* honey," I say, blocking the sun from my eyes. "That's your world record."

Just then he notices Gilbert. "Hello," he says. Then, of all things, he extends his little hand. "Tyler Moody."

Gilbert glances at me, expecting a cue, but my heart lifts so swiftly I can only shrug. What manners! Sometimes the same feeling rushes me when I hear Vince dress for work; the three smart taps of his razor on the basin can fill me with almost unbearable reassurance. In my dream, we were not traveling from Mexico, but through Russia, and I was cradling a small javelina, not Tyler.

"Pleased to know you," Gilbert says. "You're the snake man, yes?"

Tyler tips his head to his shoulder, apologetically. A small crucifix—a gift from Vince's father—hangs on the thin chain around his neck. He started wearing it the first night Vince stayed in ICU. He says, "When my dad gets out of the hospital, we're going to build a boat from a highway barrel. But not really a boat."

Gilbert nods, frowning slightly. "Hospital?"

"He has diabetes, but they just found it. I might have it, too."

"Like father, like son," Gilbert says, but nice. He and Vince are not so different. "I'm sure he'll come out fine, and you'll make your boat that's not a boat."

Tyler's hair is drying. The sun and water have bleached and puckered his skin, brought out his chicken pox scars. Once he sat on the kitchen floor and covered himself—face, pajamas, hair and feet—in butter. Gilbert says, "Call me Gil. I'm your mother's old friend."

An ostrich farmer. Vince's mother *did* leave his father, but he's not spoken of it for years. She was a dowdy, capricious woman who refused to go to the ER without making up her face. In one of our closets sits a box with her sterling and turquoise jewelry and her last wallet, still holding a lock of hair from Vince's first barber visit. What enters my mind is an old photo, pasted in an album on black construction paper, of Vince tossing seeds to an ostrich. He's tiny, wearing a bonnet that will soon come untied. The picture has always struck me as one from a vacation. Maybe that's where his mother met her lover, in Wyoming or Michigan's Upper Peninsula. I saw the album when we cleaned out her house in Sugarland, outside Houston. Tyler stayed with my parents in Corpus. He was starting to sleep by himself, and most nights I woke thinking to check on him; I worried about gas leaks and kidnappers. Two in the morning, the unfamiliar room lit by a paper-thin moon, Vince wasn't in bed. He sat in the attic, sorting ephemera. He wasn't morose but anxious, his mind and body fiending for order. He showed me his uncle's Purple Heart, telegrams sent to his mother during the war, a picture of his father—who remarkably resembled his son—standing before Niagara Falls, and the picture of himself feeding the ostrich. He mentioned nothing of his mother's infidelity, and soon I kissed his neck and led him to bed and made love to him so he could sleep.

Tyler has been talking to Gilbert, explaining the rattlesnake races in San Patricio. Hundreds of rattlers are caught on watermelon and pecan farms—though some aficionados raise their own snakes—then they race each other in chalked-off lanes. Contestants wear plastic bite guards on their shins and guide the stout-bodied snakes with aluminum poles. There is also a carnival with booths selling diamondback hatbands and paperweights and sandwiches, and clowns who paint cobras on children's faces. Tyler is ten years too young to compete, but he and his father have mounted a campaign to sidestep the restrictions; if we sign extra waivers and if Vince stays in the lane with him, they might let him enter. We're waiting to hear back.

Tyler says, "Saint Patrick led the snakes from Ireland. That's why the races are in San Patricio."

"You are the snake encyclopedia," Gilbert says. "The snake almanac."

An ease has spread between them and they're talking like old chums. Tyler moves from my feet to sit beside Gilbert. He tells him that our python, though this breed won't grow over five feet, is technically outlawed within Corpus city limits. We bought her in Southport and named her Ms. Demeanor.

"Ask your mother to drive you to San Antonio, to the Snake Farm," Gilbert says.

I kick him, hard but playful. He's flirting again—the conversational equivalent of massaging my thigh under a table. The Snake Farm is a brothel. There *are* snakes there, dozens of venomous and constrictor breeds, crammed in tanks too small and cold for them. The rub is that men ask the attendant to break a hundred-dollar bill, then get led to a double-wide behind the building, where the girls operate. Gilbert told me all of this. Before managing the Catalina, he drove a Pepsi route in San Antonio.

I'm about to shoot back some spicy, undermining answer when Tyler says, "My dad took me."

In unison, Gilbert and I say, "He did?" Then he slaps his knee and says, "A little father-son time."

"At Dad's training," Tyler says, and I remember. Vince had to attend a seminar and took Tyler for a weekend trip; I spent most of that time sunbathing beside this pool, and in Room 22. I'd not known they visited the Snake Farm and I imagine starting a fight over it later, how my not knowing will breed cattiness.

"A man got bit by a mamba," he says. "It happened that morning, but it was a dry bite."

Gilbert laughs. "Change for a hundred."

"What's a dry bite?" I ask.

"No venom," he says, as if he's already explained this. Then, brightly, to Gilbert, "Name Texas's four venomous snakes."

"Copperhead, rattlesnake, coral snake . . ." He pauses, stumped.

"Water moccasin," I say. "Cottonmouth water moccasin."

"Mother." He glares at me. "Let Gil say them."

Then he sets in asking more trivia—which is the fastest snake in the world, the most deadly? A cleaning woman shuffles into a room with an armload of towels; maybe she recognizes me, maybe not. Gilbert nods while Tyler explains that a spitting cobra can hit a predator's eyes from four yards away. My palms tingle, the way they do when an airplane lifts off, the way they did when I used to wait for Gilbert on the seafoam bedspread, naked in the television's flickering light. Dry, ragged clouds cover the sky, and a cool gray wind brings the smell of chlorine.

And suddenly I realize it: My husband has died. His heart has stopped during his nap. This hits me with a brutal, leveling clarity. They're trying to revive him right now while the three of us lounge beside the water, but it's too late; the heart monitor's spiking green line has given up. When we return to the hospital, a nurse will intercept us and I'll be ushered into a lamplit room without windows, a Bible and phone on a table between two leather chairs, across from a couch. His cardiologist will enter and my stomach will knot and I'll dash to the ladies' room to dry-heave over the toilet, realizing that Vince had always known about the ostrich farmer, as, of course, he'd known about Gilbert.

Where is Tyler in all of this? With the nurse, in the windowless room with the doctor, now joined by a priest? I simply don't see him. He's removed from me, from the earth, drowned in a motel pool or in the Gulf, or bitten by a rattlesnake or cottonmouth. His absence drains me; it contents me. Contents me because he won't have to lose his father, or me, won't have to stumble through his own mostly good marriage and bear the burden of becoming a parent and, in that same instant, a murderer. This is how I feel, like I've failed and wounded all of these men who need me, like I've chained myself to life's biggest mystery, love's trusting arrogance and its attending, inescapable regrets.

"Boa constrictor?" Gilbert offers.

Tyler stands on his heels. He hops once, then again, shaking his head. I'm sweating, the backs of my thighs stick to the chair; Gilbert sucks his toothpick.

"Python?"

"You already said that," he says. He's beaming, jumping in place, brimming with excitement. His crucifix glimmers. Does it matter if Vince had the second heart attack? Or what about the image of Tyler slathered in butter, my dream of Russia? Here's what I want to say: Truth is a coiling, slippery thing, and you can receive it any number of ways.

"Tell him, Mom," Tyler says, but then he's running and cannonballing into the pool. There is no time for me to worry that he'll slip, no chance to warn or reprimand him; his entry hardly disturbs the water. A patch of sunlight has spread over us; I can feel Gilbert growing anxious because we're alone again. I'm about to admit I don't know the answer to my son's question, about to explain the pitiable situation with Vince, but Gilbert says, "Anaconda." He says it quietly, as if he's testing the pronunciation. Then he booms it out in his full voice, "Anaconda! It's an anaconda!" Tyler starts clapping and hollering in the deep end. He's ecstatic and beautiful in the water, and when he glances at me and he's still cheering, I feel as if he's applauding me, as if something I've done is absolutely wonderful. Then, suddenly, Gilbert barrels toward the pool and jumps in, guayabera and all. His splash is huge and wasteful and some of it comes back on me. The water is warm as rain, and for a glorious moment I imagine the drought has ended.

Birds of Paradise

IN THE SUMMER OF 1974, MY FRIEND JESSE Ortega's father was hooked up with a married woman named Fancy. I was sixteen that year, living with my mother in Southport, a little fishing town north of Corpus Christi on the Gulf Coast. Down there the heat is wet and exhausting, and the land feels as wide open as the ocean. Some people in Southport ranch cattle or own farms, and a lucky few repair helicopters at the Army depot, but most men in that area haul shrimp for a living, or they work in the pits outside of town mining caliche to lay foundations and cover roads. Those are hard, solitary jobs. And when I met Fancy, there was, I think, a feeling of loneliness in all of us—my own father had disappeared by then, Jesse's mother was long buried in Colorado—and viewed in this light, with men and women afraid of untethered lives, none of what happened that afternoon seems shocking or beyond forgiveness.

Jesse's father was a man named Luis Ortega, and he had operated a bucket crane in the pits, but when I knew him, he was laid off and uninterested in returning to work. He stood six feet tall and wore western shirts with a turquoise necklace. To make money, Luis brought animals in from Mexico— snakes, monkeys, and birds, toucans and parrots and macaws. He drove a rusted-out Ford Ranger with a camper, so on those weekends when he returned from Celestun or Reynosa, he stashed what he called his "exotics" in burlap sacks and crossed the border without trouble. The animals stayed in the house until he sold them, and when I visited, the birds squawked and got wings stuck through the bars of their little cages. The monkeys threw their shit at you.

Jesse was a year older than me and had been with girls older than him. He was unlike the friends I'd had before moving to Southport, clean-cut, parochial-school boys who would have ridiculed his accent behind his back and who would have avoided making eye contact with him in gym. They would have been surprised by our friendship, would have expected me to be afraid of him, too. And I was, but I enjoyed his company because life moved faster with him and it made me feel older, more in the thick of things. Some nights after football games, he lifted Luis's keys and we took girls swimming in the pool behind the Catalina Motel. If we couldn't do that, we drove to the bay and gigged flounder and netted blue crabs. Luis would be drunk and watching Mexican wrestling by then, or passed out, or trying to recoup his losses at the dog track in Corpus, so if he entered our minds it was only to think that we didn't have to worry about him.

The day I want to describe was a Saturday in August. Jesse called early that morning—so early I suspected he'd not slept the night before—and he invited me to the beach, which I thought sounded fine. He had some girls lined up was my guess, or he wanted to catch snakes in the hummocky dunes and sell them at the pet store where Luis sometimes got rid of his birds. I told Jesse where I would be working—that summer I cleared overgrown lots for an investor—and expected him to meet me soon after I arrived, but I waited an hour before Luis's Ranger sped toward the property in front of its dust cloud. Jesse's hair was long and he wore black jeans with what my mother called his Mexican wedding shirt. She considered Jesse trouble.

"Who kept you up?" I asked. Jesse was rubbing his eyes. The air conditioner blew cold.

"Birds," he said. "We've got a house full. No one wants them right now." He eased the Ranger onto the road, then began steering with his forearm at the top of the wheel. Miles passed with only the noise of driving, the wind slicing around the truck and the dashboard rattling. The clock showed nine-fifteen and the sky was still washed in pinks and lavenders, like the soft colors inside shells.

"Luis is serious about a woman," Jesse said eventually. A row of lantana bushes streamed by, and two pump jacks, motionless and miles apart, rolled over the horizon. "She sleeps over while her husband works shifts at the refinery. She calls herself Fancy, but I doubt it's her real name."

"It could be," I said. "I went to grade school with a girl named Season."

Jesse glanced in the rearview mirror, then adjusted it. We passed a fireworks stand, just a plywood box painted red, white, and blue with faded ribbons hanging from the roof. We were traveling west, heading toward Southport.

"Luis came in my room last night." Jesse shifted in his seat. "I thought the big bastard would break my bed."

He wanted me to say something—I felt that—but I fixed my eyes outside and waited. Some grackles were scavenging in a sorghum field. Finally he said, "I pretended to sleep. Then he started talking. Not even whispering, just jabbering in his regular voice."

"What did he say?"

"He feels like he's woken up in another man's life. And he said love has no conscience. It was crazy talk. I thought maybe he was dying."

We drove under a Fourth of July banner that was still stretched over Main Street, and entered Southport. I didn't know what to say to Jesse. I saw the building where my mother and I rented an apartment above the Yellow Rose, the bar where she waitressed, and her curtains were still drawn. I assumed she'd stayed up late again, talking with her sister in San Francisco. "Maybe we'll move out there," she'd said into the phone two nights before, "and make a new start under the redwoods. I'll find a job and put Curtis in private school."

When my father left two years before, we'd moved from the Hill Country and settled in Southport to make a new start by the ocean. I'd always doubted we would stay there long, so it didn't bother me to hear my mother talking.

Jesse turned off Main Street and onto Farm Road 53, which runs south. He said, "I told Luis he was full of shit."

"Was he drunk?" I tried to picture Luis sitting in the dark, philosophizing. I'd not known him to talk much unless he was drinking, but he was not my father and I did not live with him.

"I didn't think that, but it's possible. He asked me to tell him a secret." Jesse glanced at me. "So I said I was leaving today, running away. I told him you were going, too, and we were stealing his truck."

"You said *I* was going?"

Jesse shrugged, looked out his window. The Catalina Motel came into view ahead of us, the VACANCY sign glowing faintly against the morning sky. We were nearing the string of resale shops where shrimpers hocked their belongings between good hauls.

"Luis didn't believe me," Jesse said. "He wants us to grab some things from Fancy's house, before her husband's shift ends this afternoon. It's her big getaway." Jesse didn't look at me. We were driving away from the beach and toward the port and ship channel. The smell of exhaust seeped into the cab, and caliche pelted the floorboard under my feet. "If a red Chevy's in the driveway, it belongs to her old man and we'll turn around and let Mr. Hardass handle it."

I didn't argue, because Jesse's mind was already made up. The road turned to asphalt and we continued south, with little ahead of us except puddles of heat that opened, then evaporated on the blacktop. There were cotton fields and cornfields, and the sun looked heavy, syrupy—it warmed my face and arm through the window, and my eyes started getting drowsy as we drove. We passed a few cars, but mostly the road was quiet. Jesse gunned the engine and swerved at some seagulls on the shoulder, then he laughed when I grabbed the dashboard. Eventually a little house emerged on the horizon and it seemed nice from the distance, but when we were upon it, the windows were boarded over and I saw that no one had lived there in a long time.

THE NEIGHBORHOODS ALONG THE SHIP CHANNEL are poor and neglected, mostly small tract houses rented by servicemen or Vietnamese shrimpers or families who cannot afford anything better. The air conditioner had quit on us, and I smelled the rotten-egg odor of the oil refineries across the bay, where Fancy's husband worked. We drove slowly and looked for a street called Lucille. Jesse's mood was sour, though I also believed the idea of breaking into Fancy's thrilled him. I was not excited about it. I hoped that we would see the red Chevy at Fancy's house and step away from whatever was poised to happen, but when we found it, her narrow seashell driveway was empty and Jesse steered in.

The front door was unlocked and when Jesse opened it, cold air rolled out of the house the way it rolls out of motel rooms—I could hear a window unit humming. The living room was clean, furnished with a couch and chair and television; it smelled lemony. A brass-framed mirror and a painting of some mallards hung on the walls, but there was nothing else, and the sparseness made it seem like a space where people slept but did not live. I felt giant in that little room, as though my slightest movement would shake the house. Jesse slipped into the hall saying, "Hello. Hello." I thought to wait in the truck, but didn't want to go outside alone.

Jesse began rummaging through the rooms, opening and closing drawers and closets, while I sat at Fancy's kitchen table. A stack of bills addressed to Phillip Bundick lay across from me, as well as a scrapbook someone had been filling. The pictures were from the beach, mostly of a dark-haired woman wading with a little girl wearing blow-up arm floats. The woman looked too young to be the girl's mother, maybe only a few years older than me or Jesse. She was pretty, with a heart-shaped face, and in one photo, her nipples, small and dark, showed beneath her white bathing suit. In another shot, a man held a dead rabbit over a campfire, and below the picture were the words "Bunny cooks a bunny," written in a woman's looping, optimistic script.

"I can't find her jewelry," Jesse said. He opened the refrigerator behind me, throwing a triangle of light over the table and pictures. "But I packed a bag of her clothes. And he's set with guns and knives. We could pawn them in Corpus."

"We're too young. They wouldn't let us."

Jesse closed the refrigerator and the light over the pictures vanished. He pressed a beer can to his forehead, rolled it across his brow then back again. He said, "You know all the impossibilities."

"Maybe she hides the jewelry from her husband," I said.

"Maybe *he* hid it from us."

Jesse opened the beer and the snap of the tab cracked through the house. The small bag he'd stuffed with Fancy's clothes lay inside the hall and after a swallow of beer, he unzipped it and removed a pink negligee. He pinched it by the lacy straps, as if it disgusted him. "How's this?"

"It smells like strawberries," I said. Seeing the teddy made me feel like a child, and I wanted to leave. "We should get going."

"It suits her," he said. Jesse wiped his face on the satin, then crammed it back in the duffel. "She's fruity."

He leaned close to the table, peering at the picture showing the woman's nipples. I smelled the beer and his sweat.

"That's her," he said. Then after another pull from the can, he added, "More or less."

I didn't know what that meant, but didn't care to ask, and Jesse disappeared into the back of the house again. I thought he was getting a little drunk, that maybe he'd been drinking earlier that morning, and that we would not go to the beach. I studied the picture again. I wondered what Fancy had been thinking right then, if she knew Luis yet or if this was a happier time in the life with her husband. She wasn't smiling in the photo, which made me believe she hadn't wanted the picture snapped at all.

Ten minutes passed before Jesse came down the hall with Fancy's jewelry box, a little black hutch with an Oriental dragon slithering across its lid. Something made me believe he'd found it earlier, though I couldn't say what that was. "Let's go see Luis," he said. "We'll bring this back early and collect a reward."

"Okay," I said, maybe too quickly, and stood up. "What about the beach?"

"We'll go later. I want you to see her. She cooks naked."

I shut the scrapbook and thought I wouldn't mind seeing Fancy's body, but I supposed she never cooked that way and Jesse was only saying words.

"She brought some shark meat over yesterday. They're grilling it tonight. You're invited." Jesse placed the jewelry box on the counter and surveyed the kitchen, as if he'd lost something. He leaned against the wall. A car passed outside, then when its noise died away, I heard the din of the refrigerator and crickets trilling in the yard. I thought we would have left by then.

"I *could* run away today," Jesse said. He made a fist, then fanned his fingers. "I've thought about it."

"Everyone has."

"The world is different than we think," he said. His eyes caught something behind me—maybe his reflection in the brass mirror—and he asked, "How old do I look?"

"Seventeen," I said. "You're seventeen."

"If you didn't know me, how old would I be?" He puffed out his chest, straightened his posture.

"I don't know," I said. "I'm not good at this."

"I could pass for twenty or twenty-one and enlist right now." Jesse's chin and cheeks were smooth, so he looked like a boy, not even a young man of his age, and I thought the recruiters would laugh if he tried fooling them. "When I get a pilot's license," he said, "I'll fly my jet under bridges."

"I've heard of that," I lied.

"Luis is 4-F," he said. "It means he's more harm than good." Saying that seemed to satisfy him, and I sensed we were about to head out when he added, "I hate the fucking beach. I never want to go again."

A quality I'd not heard before, a rawness, weighted Jesse's voice. "Okay," I said. "That's fine."

"If I ran away, I'd go somewhere without water." Jesse raised his eyes to me, then gazed into the front room with its few pieces of furniture. "Somewhere where the earth is solid." And I realized Jesse wasn't drunk at all, but that he hated Fancy for staying in his house and hated his father for being his father and that maybe he hated me because he knew I saw that. I was glad not to be Jesse then, and it relieved me when he pushed himself away from the wall and started outside.

We drove with our windows down and the landscape inched by without change—dry, yellow fields running alongside the two-lane road. To the east, smoke from a scorched crop lingered against the rock-white horizon. We were heading north. Neither of us spoke much during the drive, though eventually I said, "I'd go somewhere with snow."

———

PHILLIP BUNDICK'S RED CHEVY SAT IN JESSE'S driveway, the driver's door yawning open. When I saw it, I swallowed, heard the muscles roll and contract in my throat. Jesse muttered something in Spanish that I couldn't understand. He braked—I remember how softly he pressed the pedal—but let the truck roll forward and parked on the road a short distance from the house. His eyes stayed on the house. A window fan propped open the front door, but from our view it was impossible to see inside.

"We should call someone," I said.

Jesse rubbed the back of his neck, something he did when he got nervous, and cut the ignition. He stashed Fancy's jewelry box under his seat, something I wouldn't have thought to do, and pushed the duffel behind my heels. "Go call someone," Jesse said. "Maybe your mother or the cavalry or the President." Then he was hopping the ditch and crossing his yard. He stepped onto his porch without hesitating and went inside the house and out of my vision.

The engine pinged and clicked as it cooled. A boy and girl who lived next door to Jesse rode past on bicycles, locks of sweaty hair clinging to their foreheads. They had grown since I last saw them. The girl stood and started pedaling hard, then the boy raced after her and they were gone. I tried to recall when I'd last ridden a bicycle but couldn't, could hardly remember learning to ride one. I thought of my mother, wondered if she'd woken yet. If she was awake, I hoped she was visiting with one of her friends or watching her soap operas and not worrying about me. Then I climbed from the truck, eased my door closed, and started for the house.

"Who the Jesus are you?" Phillip Bundick said when I appeared in the door. He was holding Luis against the wall with a black snub-nosed pistol pressed into his throat. For a moment the only part of my body was my heart, pumping so hard I felt it inside my head. Jesse stood just inside the threshold facing his father and Phillip Bundick, while Fancy sat on the couch, her knees bent to tuck her feet beside her. Her hair was blond now, unbrushed, and her hands covered her eyes. She wore a red silk kimono with a yellow dragon embroidered on the shoulder. Fancy looked recently woken; she and Luis both did; he wasn't wearing a shirt. Phillip Bundick stomped his boot and the house rattled—the framed needlepoints on the wall, the table in front of Fancy and the empty bottles on it, the windows. A bird screeched in another room.

Phillip Bundick pushed the gun deeper into the fat under Luis's jaw, which made him flatten his palms against the paneling. "Well," he said and cut his eyes at me again.

"He's my friend," Jesse said. "He's meeting me here to go crabbing."

"Have you been in my house, too?" Phillip Bundick leaned his weight into Luis and stomped again, twice.

I opened my mouth to speak, without any idea how to answer, but Fancy said, "What difference does that make now, Bunny?" She raised her head from her hands, wiped her eyes, and momentarily the only sounds were her sniffling and the fan in the front door.

"Because I'm not accustomed to men gallivanting through my house unless I've invited them," he said. He twisted his neck, then focused on Luis's chest, pale and hairless, like another stomach. Luis stood on his tiptoes to try and gain some leverage, but soon he relaxed. Then without turning his head, Phillip Bundick found me with his eyes. "Do you know your friend's father makes a habit of putting his pecker in places it doesn't belong?"

"Oh, Christ, Bunny," Fancy said. Jesse glanced at her as if she'd spoken out of turn. My hands felt heavy at my sides, as awkward as boxing gloves, and I wanted to cross them behind my back, but stayed still.

"Well," Phillip Bundick said in a defeated tone, "you should know that about him. And my wife is recently one of those places."

"They're just babies," Fancy said. At another time, I thought she would have made a scene and stormed from the room, but Phillip Bundick twisted his fist and turned his knuckles against Luis's throat and Fancy did not move. He didn't look violent. His arm shook from the pressure it took to hold Luis that way, and I thought he probably enjoyed his wife calling him Bunny, that maybe she was the only person in the world who called him that. Phillip and Fancy Bundick, it occurred to me, were much older than I'd imagined and the pictures on their table were from years before; I did not know who the little girl might be. Phillip Bundick seemed about to say something then, maybe to Luis or Fancy or to himself, but he just clenched his jaw and squinted his eyes. His face flushed. Then he rammed Luis between the legs with his knee. It was a short, solid blow, and Luis buckled.

"Why don't we stop this now?" Jesse said. He took a step forward and sounded more angry than afraid, which surprised me, because it seemed everyone was afraid then, even Phillip Bundick.

"What a beautiful idea," Fancy said. "Doesn't that sound just beautiful, Bunny?"

"I wish to God this would've never gotten started on me," he said in a loud, wild voice. Phillip Bundick heaved his shoulder and body against Luis to keep him standing. "I wish I hadn't learned about this."

Luis was clutching his stomach and gasping as though there weren't enough air in the room. Phillip Bundick appeared about to kick him again, but said, "I feel like I've already died."

Luis groaned. Sweat had beaded on his face and forehead, and when he squirmed against the wall, Jesse raised his hands and laced his fingers behind his neck. "Okay. Okay. That's good now. Why don't we let him rest a while? He could use some water."

Phillip Bundick turned to Jesse then, studying him in a slow and measured way. I could hear him breathing through his nose with his mouth shut, but he was regaining his composure. "Your old man takes a good punch. He'll come out of this fine. That's what he's thinking right now. Isn't it?" His eyes moved from Jesse to Luis. He leaned within an inch of Luis's face. "You're thinking this will all end soon and you'll just find another lady to work your magic on. This is just a regular day for you, right?"

"This isn't regular for anyone, Bunny," Fancy said. "Not even us. Let's get in the car and drive home. Okay? We can talk tonight. I'll grill your shark for you." It sounded as though she might continue, maybe add that things between them would work out or that she loved him and didn't love Luis, but Fancy just closed her mouth. She shook her head and scanned the room without letting her eyes rest on any one thing.

And what Phillip Bundick did then was take a step back, then another and another, and simply walk away. He glanced at Fancy and Luis as if he were lost, but then turned and shouldered past Jesse and me. I expected something to happen, for Luis or even Jesse to tackle Phillip Bundick or hit him from behind. Maybe he wanted to be hurt, so he left himself open, but we watched him go down the porch steps without harm. Before he climbed into the Chevy, Phillip Bundick looked at the sky—it was a hard blue then—then he lowered his eyes to the house. I felt he would make some statement, and was waiting to hear his voice when he lifted his arm and fired the pistol three times into the air. And after that, he was gone.

LONELINESS CAN LEAD PEOPLE THE SAME WAY THAT love can, and sometimes to the same places, so that inside the cheerless situation where you never wanted to find yourself, it can seem impossible to distinguish one from the other. Maybe Luis felt that in Jesse's room the night before, and maybe Phillip Bundick felt it as his Chevy topped the hill that afternoon and he disappeared from our sight. Such feelings have surfaced in my life since then, but at sixteen being in love and being alone existed as opposites in my mind, though that, of course, is dead wrong.

The officer who came to Jesse's house that afternoon was short and young, and despite the muscles bulging under his uniform, he seemed jittery talking with Luis in the driveway. Jesse and I had carted the birds and their cages to the storage shed behind the house, because Luis suspected the neighbors would call the police about the gunshots. He had splashed water on his face and hair, and now wore a tank top and boots. Fancy had changed into a yellow sundress, and as she spoke with the officer, Luis tucked in his shirt.

"Son," Luis called. "Son, let's talk with the police now." Jesse jogged across the yard. The afternoon heat was coming on then, but a breeze was blowing and I found some shade on the porch. Fancy eventually shook the officer's hand and came to sit on the bench beside me. She had brushed her hair and put on makeup, and a thin gold chain with a little cross pendant hung around her neck.

"What is today?" she asked.

"Saturday," I said. The officer jotted down something Jesse had told him. Luis shot a glance at us on the porch.

"Then I hate Saturdays," Fancy said. We were on a swing made for two people. I wondered if I stank from riding in the hot truck. "Southport," she said, as though contemplating the name. "Where you're either drunk or fishing."

"We're moving," I said. The words sounded strange in my voice. "My aunt lives in California. We'll stay with her and I'll go to a private school."

"I acted in a movie once." Fancy started peeling flakes of paint from her armrest, watching her hands. Stubble peppered her calves, though that didn't bother me. "Actually, I was an extra in a crowd scene, but we filmed for three days. At the time I had red hair, like an orange, but on the last day of shooting I overslept, so they had to redo the whole scene without me because the director couldn't match my hair color. Something like that. He said I'd cost him twenty-eight thousand dollars, so I guess that's what I'm worth. At least I'm not cheap."

I recalled Fancy's pictures and realized she had been wading in the Pacific Ocean, not the Gulf. She seemed mysterious then, like someone who knew things I would never know. I said, "I saw your photo album on the table."

"Did you?" She smiled at me and seemed flattered. "Picture's worth a thousand words I'll never say, right?"

I shrugged, and though it surprised me as much as anyone, I said, "I'd like to be a reporter. I'd like to tell about people doing important things." I'd hoped Fancy would respond, encourage me or say something else to make me feel good, but a voice crackled through the cruiser's radio and we stayed quiet while the officer reached for his CB.

"They've caught poor Bunny," she said.

"I didn't hear that."

"Neither did I, but that's what happened. I'm his wife, I know." Fancy dropped a sliver of paint and ran her thumb over her short fingernails.

"Is that your real name? Fancy?"

She squinted at me, not angrily but as if she were assessing a flaw in my character. I held her eyes for only a second, though it felt like a long time before she turned away. Jesse and Luis stood beside each other, with their backs against the cruiser, while the officer sat inside talking on the radio. A wind blew and I heard branches scratching against the side of the house. I wished I'd kept quiet about Fancy's name. She said, "He intended to be a priest, Luis did. You wouldn't know that now, I guess."

Luis and Jesse chuckled about something, and seeing them that way made me think of Luis sitting on Jesse's bed the night before. I wondered if he knew about Luis wanting to be a priest.

"He wants to start a legitimate bird business. Birds of Paradise he would call it. And those needlepoints on the walls, the sand dollars and clowns and that woman walking in the garden—he does those when he can't sleep. He's proud of them."

"They're nice," I said, though I'd never really examined them or considered Luis being proud of anything.

"The officer is a friend of mine's son. He doesn't know me, though. His mother is older and has cancer. He'll see a lot worse than this in his life."

And because it seemed right, I said, "We all will."

"Or have," Fancy said. Then after a moment, "Do you want to hear the saddest thing I've ever seen?"

"Yes," I said. I liked Fancy's voice.

"I took a cruise in the Caribbean, off the coast of St. Lucia, and I watched all these rich people throw change to the natives. Maybe a hundred of them floated out on little boats and old surfboards. It's a tradition there." Fancy stood and smoothed her dress against the backs of her thighs. "After the money ran out, they started yelling for fruit. 'Fruit! Give us fruit!'" She quieted her voice, but raised her eyes and waved her arms as if she were far below, in the ocean. "And sure enough they started throwing fruit to them. Bananas, oranges, lemons, but away from the boat to watch them fetch it. Some kids climbed to the higher decks and tried to bean them with apples. They hit one man, an old bald man with skinny, skinny arms, and he went under." She touched her hair, rolled strands between her thumb and fingers. "I just stayed in my cabin after that, crying."

"I'm sorry," I said. I raised my eyes toward the cruiser, trying to think of something horrible to confide to Fancy. I remembered only what Jesse had said about my just knowing impossibilities, but right then it sounded less than horrible.

"I dated a doctor before Bunny. We weren't in love." Fancy glanced at me, smiled, then pursed her lips. She exhaled. "Being alone isn't my strong suit."

Then Jesse was strolling across the yard. Fancy straightened herself on the bench, and when he came close enough to hear, she asked, "What's the verdict?"

"He doesn't need to speak with Curtis," he said. "But you're going to prison. Forever." He smirked at Fancy and she touched her cheek, then started fingering her cross, gazing away from him. Jesse raised his eyes to me, urging me to laugh or smile, but I only shook my head. He seemed a stranger to me then, and I wanted him to leave us alone. And maybe Jesse recognized that because he was stepping backward across the yard when he said, "That's the verdict. That's how all of this ends. Maybe Curtis will visit you on your birthday."

He turned and walked toward the Ranger with his father watching. After a moment Luis stole a look at Fancy, but averted his eyes when she noticed. Whatever had existed between them, I knew, was finished, and I saw that Luis wished things were different. I doubted Phillip Bundick had intended to shoot him, but only to scare him and make him feel sorry for things. I did not know how he learned we'd been in his house or that Fancy was with Luis—possibly someone told him, possibly Fancy herself communicated it, though without words or voice—or maybe he just had a feeling that turned out to be true. I thought the possibility of Fancy's leaving had eaten at him for some time and he had simply lost his sanity trying to stop the inevitable, which will drive anyone crazy. Already, I felt detached from them, as if I'd left Southport and was living in California near the redwood forest, where they would not make a difference in my life's unfolding. Maybe no one would.

"And yes." Fancy paused as Jesse tried cranking the ignition. "It *is* my real name. I also have two sisters, Mary and Arden, but who knows where they are."

I said, "It's a pretty name."

Fancy smiled a weak smile at me, then took my hand and ducked under my arm so that I held her like a little girl. Jesse continued to turn the engine, but it wouldn't catch, and soon Luis and the officer raised the hood and checked for the trouble. It was only the middle of the day, though it seemed late. Clouds had blown in and canopied that hard blue sky and I thought it might rain. I imagined Jesse enlisting in the Army soon, and maybe flying his plane under bridges. I imagined us as grown men, worlds apart, realizing that we'd forged our friendship out of necessity and availability and the violent knowledge that it wouldn't last, and realizing too that such alliances are not necessarily tragic. Anything seemed possible to me then, and it gave me the floating feeling you get when you're in a dark room and although everything is black, you suddenly realize your eyes are open. Fancy pressed her face to my shoulder, then relaxed, and I wondered what was on her mind. Maybe she was thinking of acting in a movie, or about her sisters or splashing in the Pacific Ocean, or about when she would next see Phillip Bundick. Or maybe she thought this: We are not responsible for other people, cannot be responsible for them. It was not a crazy thought, or unique or sad, just one that can occur in life, whether you're young or old, alone or in love. Her breathing slowed. I thought she might be falling asleep, and I didn't want to wake her. At that moment I felt content, and I only wanted to let Fancy's body rest against mine, for her to feel the breeze on her skin, in her blond hair, and for both of us to stay still and, however briefly, close our eyes in the shade.

Buy for Me the Rain

ON THE WARM JANUARY MORNING WHEN LEI-
land Marshall buried his mother, he kept shifting in
his folding chair, hoping to see Moira Jarrett. Her flight was
scheduled to land before the service started, but even as the
line of mourners filed by the casket, she hadn't arrived. This
was in Corpus Christi, at a cemetery near the ocean, under a
canvas tent that gave everything a green hue. Death had come
for his mother's body in the night, had come with miserable
slowness, but when women in the line asked, he said she had
passed peacefully in her sleep. As he spoke, he glanced over
their shoulders for Moira. He watched for her as the mourners dispersed, then again when they brought sympathy and
snack platters to the house. She never showed. Soon his
mother's friends slipped into their dainty coats, collected
purses and jangled keys, and Lee found himself under the
ashen, thickening sky, waving as the last car pulled away
from the curb.

Russell Jarrett, Moira's older brother, stayed longer than the others. He stepped outside carrying a garbage bag.

Lee said, "Those women had a good time today."

"And a few beers. It's worse than a Super Bowl party in there."

Lee had returned from St. Louis a year before, leaving a job teaching eleventh-grade history to stay with his mother while she underwent treatment, then when that failed, to care for her as she died. On the day of the funeral, all of it seemed part of another person's life, a story he'd read in the *Caller-Times*. He was thirty-three and, now, an orphan.

After Russell set the bag on the curb, Lee asked, "Any word from Moira?"

"Flight's delayed," he said. "She'll be here for dinner. She's sorry about missing everything."

Lee hoped Russell would say more, but didn't want to press. Moira, he knew, was flying from London, where she worked with a dance company, but otherwise her current life remained a mystery. He wondered how England suited her, if she intended to relocate permanently. Except for crossing into Mexico, Lee had never been out of the country—a fact that, like his mother's cancer, he seemed to always be avoiding. He wondered if Moira was traveling alone.

The wind gusted, stripping more leaves from the Chinese tallow. Lee thought to open the windows in the house and start airing out the rooms, then he realized that could be done in an hour or a month; the rushing was over. He said, "I still haven't gone into the den."

"Why should you?" Russell said. "If you need something from there, I'll get it."

"That room doesn't even seem part of the house right now. I can hardly picture it."

Russell untucked his shirt and trained his eyes on a beagle barking down the street. He sold life insurance—he'd written the policy for Lee's mother years before—and regularly interacted with grieving clients, but he was unaccustomed to consoling Lee. For the last three nights, he'd insisted that Lee sleep at his apartment, and too often in that time he had guaranteed that her insurance papers were in order; he could offer no other relief. Having mentioned the den galled Lee. He'd forgotten his role, had forgotten to chaperone the conversation, because, really, the day seemed too unremarkable, lacking in weight and ballast, to hold his mother's funeral; the lawn needed raking; a tire on her Oldsmobile was flat; Moira, as usual, was late.

Russell had been talking, but Lee only heard him say, "Or maybe you feel relieved. No fault in that."

"I feel hungry." And though he'd meant only to lighten Russell's mood, Lee realized he *was* hungry. It was just past two, the hour when he should've been warming her soup or pouring her cereal.

"They drank the beer but spared the food," Russell said. "Eat, then take a nap. Try to relax—that's what she would want."

That made sense. Of course he should rest today, yet the idea hadn't occurred to him. Immediately his body started surrendering to the promise of unconsciousness, as if he'd taken one of his mother's sedatives; it was a buoyant feeling, the sense that the worst lay behind him.

Russell said, "When you get up, Moira will be here."

"She'll regale us with stories."

A car with a Christmas wreath tied to its grill turned onto the street, and the driver, a neighbor who hadn't attended the funeral, saluted solemnly.

Lee said, "I think she would've liked the service."

"Absolutely. The flowers, the music, all of her beer-grubbing friends. She'd be proud."

"No," Lee said, "I meant Moira."

MEN COULDN'T GET MOIRA OUT OF THEIR SYS-tems. "Like herpes," she'd once said. For three months after she'd broken a lawyer's heart, he left packages on her porch—flowers, chocolate, a white-gold choker, opal earrings; occasionally she'd had to change phone numbers because old flames refused to stop calling. Lee himself could hardly recall a time when he wasn't pining for her. When he had been nothing more than her brother's watchful friend, he'd envied and judged her suitors—young men with long hair and older men with money, a woman who sang jazz, and later, briefly, the singer's husband. His heart thrilled when she dismissed them, though he knew she was beyond him, too. Her wispy clothes smelled of marijuana and incense—pungent teases of her other, more essential and alluring life; she made oblique references to a past pregnancy; someone, an affronted spouse or jilted lover, had twice broken her car windows.

The second time was in front of Lee's mother's house. That year, between college and grad school, he'd started finding Moira on his arm, in his bed. He spent nights convincing himself the relationship would last, but Moira left him bewitched and small-feeling, and he always knew she would not grow to need him. The shattered windows evidenced a past and future in which he didn't figure.

A Saturday morning, they stood barefoot on the sunblanched lawn. Lee's mother had left a note saying she'd gone shopping, but he knew she was at the cemetery, grooming his father's grave.

Moira said, "Everything happens to me twice."

She liked saying this, had said it before. She was referring to jail and lightning; she'd been arrested twice, once for unpaid tickets, once for petty larceny, for stealing a mink stole from Dillard's. And twice she'd been struck by lightning, in a sorghum field and beside a pool; she'd been on the early news. Now, the busted windows.

"Things rarely happen to me, even once."

"So we're a good fit."

He touched the small of her back, felt the knuckles of her spine. He wondered if his mother had seen the broken glass before leaving, if she'd resisted knocking on his door because she didn't want to spy Moira wrapped in the striped comforter she'd bought him in high school. She viewed Moira as a reckless, wayward flower child, and had probably deceived herself into thinking the car belonged to a neighbor.

A joke occurred to him: "Maybe my mother broke them."

"To dissuade me from corrupting her son." She slitted her eyes, smirked darkly. An hour earlier, as his mother washed dishes, Moira'd had to bite the edge of the blanket to muffle her moaning. Now, she held the hem of her T-shirt (his, actually), threatening to flash the traffic. She liked flashing people.

"We should turn her in."

Looking at the street, Moira said, "The villain always returns to the scene of the crime."

His mother's Oldsmobile eased into the driveway. She cut the ignition (the engine cycled a second or two longer) and lowered the windows an inch. Then she opened the door, said hello and embraced Moira. Lee watched his mother's eyes close, as if she were hearing adverse news; she didn't look at him. He tried to determine if she'd been crying at the cemetery, or if it had been more of an angry morning, but he couldn't tell.

Moira said, "Lee thinks you broke my windows."

His mother eyed the damage, then smiled. She said, "Mama didn't raise no fool son."

They laughed, though Lee felt a rising commotion in his chest. After another glance at the shattered windows, his mother said, "Now, Mr. Detective, grab my groceries from the trunk."

HE HAD SPENT CHRISTMAS DAY BESIDE THE HOSPITAL bed that crowded his mother's small den. He'd adorned the bed's guardrails with red tinsel, but she never noticed. The metastasis had claimed her mind months before, stripped her to a husk of body and voice; in October, she'd sobbed and cursed him because he refused to take her trick-or-treating. Now she mostly slept. When she woke Christmas afternoon, he spooned broth into her mouth and wiped her chin. She smiled, then submitted to a sponge bath. Always there was the suppressed, aching hope that such coherence—when she remembered his name or her own, when she spoke lucidly, or watched television and not the ceiling fan—signaled some improvement the oncologists could not predict. But when he tried to comb her hair, she screamed; she mistook the brush for a pistol.

A year before, they had driven three hours south and spent the holiday in the Rio Grande Valley and Mexico. They left early to avoid the afternoon heat—even in December, temperatures climb into the nineties. They dallied at rest areas and fruit stands, watched deer graze in the shade of mesquite trees. "Too bad we don't have anything to feed them," she said. Across the border, she bought half-priced leather purses and cartons of cigarettes, a sequined serape, and a Santa Claus–shaped piñata for a neighbor's daughter. *Farmacias* anchored almost every corner, and she haggled with girls in dingy lab coats about the prices of muscle relaxers and Procrit. Lee trailed his fingers over the metal shelves where pill bottles were stacked in pyramids; the Spanish labels and dusty surfaces made him feel nervous, illicit. They ate dinner above the Canada Store and after the enchiladas, she drank margaritas—the best she'd ever tasted, she kept saying on the ride home. She was fifty-three. In a week she would start chemo.

"I wonder if it will hurt," she said. "Or if I'll just throw up."

"The doctor said some people don't even get sick. You could be one of those."

She lowered her window, which meant she needed a cigarette. The scratch of her lighter, a flash of flame. He thought she might say something after blowing a breath of smoke into the night, but miles ticked by with only the sound of wind slicing around the car. The mucky air smelled of brine, like the Spanish moss draping the trees. Eventually the headlights started illuminating plastic grocery bags caught on barbed-wire fences.

"Those belonged to illegals," his mother said. She flicked her cigarette outside and rolled up her window. "The bags keep their valuables dry when they cross the river."

She reclined the seat, bent her elbow over her eyes. Though he hadn't realized it was on, Lee could now hear the radio, the speakers whispering an old song, something by the Nitty Gritty Dirt Band. She said, "I wonder what they bring. What would you bring?"

Before he could answer—when he was still imagining the men and women and children fording the river—she said, "I know. You'd take pictures of your girlfriends. And one of Dad. Maybe some books, but they'd get heavy."

"And you. I'd take a picture of you."

She patted his thigh. "Merry Christmas."

"Merry Christmas," he said. He tried tuning the radio, but the reception had faded.

Then she was sitting up, saying, "Daddy was so smart, Lee. He told me about the illegals and their little bags." She shook out another cigarette, lit it, and cranked down her window again. "I thought he was fooling me, lying in the yard like that. I'd brought him water, you know."

He nodded. "I know."

"He'd be so ashamed of me. I've made a mess of everything."

"Don't be silly, Mama," he said. What he believed, though, was that his father would be disappointed, as he himself sometimes was. Since she had run screaming to his father's body years before, she had quit jobs, stripped the walls of his pictures, abandoned her evening walks to sit in the den chain-smoking. Loss had become her religion; in her attempts to conceal her grief, she had worn it the way other women wore wedding rings.

Lee said, "We've had a fine day. You're doing swell. I'm proud of you."

"Leiland, I know what happens." She paused to clear her throat, but started hacking hard enough to spill ashes onto the door panel. Her cough was wet and rattling; he cringed. He slowed the car and eased onto the shoulder, but she shook her head and waved him on.

After the spell passed, she said, "I know what happens. I'll lose my hair and vomit and ruin your life. Then I'll still die."

"You're not going to die, Mama," he said. "You'll beat this."

She drew on her cigarette, then let a stream of smoke slip from the side of her mouth. Ahead, a line of cars was backed up at the Sarita checkpoint. The delay would add an hour to the drive, at least.

"Lee," she said, "I don't want to beat it."

HIS MOST RECENT LOVER WAS A FLAXEN-HAIRED librarian in St. Louis, but the relationship had petered out before he returned to Corpus. When he'd bought his ticket a year before, he'd thought, sheepishly and irrationally, of seeing Moira. Then Russell explained about London, the job coordinating rehearsals. For months, Lee tried to shut out her presence, but even the glomming heat of the Coastal Bend seemed to share her scent. With Moira, he'd always felt his real life was waiting right around the corner and if he could just keep up, she'd lead him to it.

ON THE NIGHT OF THE FUNERAL, SHE TOOK A LIMO to Russell's apartment—"Why take cabs? For ten dollars more you get a town car," she said, then disappeared into the bathroom. Lee'd not seen her in five years. A discomposed feeling, almost like fervor, came over him as she showered, but when she emerged wearing baggy jeans and one of Russell's button-downs, he was more relaxed. Moira's hair dripped onto her shoulders, and she looked heavier than he'd remembered or imagined. And at once, just how often he'd imagined their reunion became clear. The scene had played out countless ways in his mind, yet sitting across from Moira at Russell's table seemed unreal, a dream he couldn't shake after waking. She dribbled the last of the wine into their glasses, and spoke of spending New Year's Eve in a charter plane, flying over fireworks. She said, "They looked like a school of tiny fish or a giant octopus."

"A starving octopus will eat his own heart," Russell blurted. He waggled his glass in a mock toast, his eyes glassy, slow. "I learned that in college."

Moira said, "Russ? Sweetie? How much have you drunk today?"

"Not enough."

"A gang of old women swiped his beer."

"My New Year's resolution," Russell said, "is to never fly in a plane with octopi."

Moira cackled, a laugh that started small then opened up and pushed against the dining room walls. Russell seemed unduly offended, so she offered a coy apology. Then she winked at Lee. He said, "My resolution is to find another bottle of wine."

How odd, absurd really, to be looking for Chardonnay in Russell's cabinets. After his father's funeral, Lee had spent the night watching his mother sleep in his recliner, fearing she'd taken more Valium than she admitted. He woke her every two hours. The vigil gave substance, direction to the time. And since then, part of his identity had been attending to her, attempting, even when her health appeared solid, to raise her spirits and assuage her loneliness. He'd invented excuses to call from Missouri, bought airline tickets whenever the prices dropped, counseled her against books and films that might depress her. He couldn't recall not worrying about her, couldn't imagine not worrying in the future. Who was he if not a distant, overprotective son? In Russell's kitchen, everything felt random and unmoored. The light seemed too grainy, the creak of the cupboard hinges too shrill. The wine was not where he remembered.

At the table, Moira was laughing again. "That's ludicrous, Russell."

"It's true." He smiled drowsily. "Lee, buddy, how tall are you?"

"Five-nine," Lee said, though suddenly the answer seemed wrong, a random number he'd plucked from the ether. "Maybe a little shorter."

Russell shrugged, saying, "Well, you *look* tall."

"Anyway," Moira said, "the short man only paid half price, maybe twenty American dollars. I got in free because I'm a woman, but most men paid forty bucks."

Russell repeated, "Forty bucks," chuckling. The alcohol was thickening his tongue, blotching his cheeks.

"What are we talking about?"

"She's regaling us with stories!"

Moira continued, "There were red tube lights hanging from the ceiling, and each room had a sofa, leather or velvet. One had a Jacuzzi. But no doors anywhere. You just walked from room to room, stepping over them." She paused. She glanced at Lee, then Russell, then Lee again. Water trickled in the rain gutter. She said, "People fucking everywhere."

Russell slapped his knee. "Christ on the cross!"

Moira sipped her wine, swallowed quickly. Excitement brightened her eyes. She said, "Waitresses walked around selling chocolate and condoms. I tried not to stare, but that was silly because they *want* you to stare. People you never think of having sex. A deaf woman did sign language to the man on top of her."

"And this place is legal?" Lee asked.

"Completely. It's sleazy and fabulous. You feel—"

"Jesus, Moira," Russell interrupted. He slouched forward, his expression blank. "You didn't."

She narrowed her eyes, then shifted to face the picture window. The night had turned the glass to a mirror and Lee saw her staring into the darkness. The rain fell heavier now. His mother's plot would be soaked, the sod filling the hole turned to mud. Moira drew her leg up to sit on her calf.

"Of course not, Russell."

They glared at each other for a moment, then Russell refilled his glass. Moira folded her napkin, aligned the edges and smoothed the creases. The heater cycled on.

When no one spoke, Lee asked, "How long can the octopus live without its heart?"

HE HAD BEEN IN THE FRONT ROOM, WAITING FOR the hospice worker to return to the phone, when his mother began calling his name from the den. He was still glum and frustrated from trying to get her to take her morning medication. She'd been feisty, opening and closing her mouth too quickly for him to place the capsule on her tongue, then once he succeeded, she refused to swallow; she smiled and spit the pill onto her nightgown. Eventually she'd cooperated and when she slept, he crept into the kitchen to arrange delivery of another oxygen canister. It was only October, but November's supply was already exhausted. He'd been on hold for ten minutes, listening to elevator music in the receiver.

"Lee," she called. Her voice was bright but diminished, a sliver of its old self. "Lee."

"Just a minute," he said.

She didn't need help to the restroom; he'd taken her before her nap. Probably she needed another pack of cigarettes or wanted help lighting one she already had. Recently she'd started forgetting how to smoke. He found her puffing on straws and ballpoint pens, and because it did more good than harm, he left her alone. Withholding her cigarettes allowed him to believe she might live another day, another hour, just as staying on the phone rather than rushing to her side seemed reasonable.

The sound of her fall reminded him of something being dropped into sand. He burst down the hallway, then stopped short of the den's threshold for fear of planting his foot on her body. She wasn't there. His eyes scanned the den—the linen that needed changing, the flowers, the couch and television, her recliner, all of the sharp, hard corners that could hurt her. The room was empty.

Then he saw them; her oxygen tubes pulled taut from the machine, stretching through the sliding doors onto the sundeck. Everything stopped. Through the glass, he saw her feet and legs, hopelessly tangled in the tubing. The sun shone bright on her body, illuminating pale, dry thighs. Her left hand still clutched her nightgown; he pictured her inching toward the deck, holding the hem above her ankles so she wouldn't stumble. A cigarette and her lighter lay a few feet away. His heart flattened: blood. It saturated a lock of her hair and dripped down to collect in a spreading, syrupy puddle. She was not crying or speaking or doing anything at all; her eyes were locked on the potted azalea in front of her.

"Mama," he said, trying to calm the panic in his voice. "Mama, are you okay?"

When she didn't answer, he thought, *This is how it happened, this is where you found her.* Months before, they had come onto the sundeck when her hair started falling out, and he shaved her head, first with clippers, then a razor. She had said she felt like a recruit going to boot camp.

"Mama," he said. "Mama, it's Lee."

She blinked, then blinked again, and smacked her lips, as if just waking. He exhaled. The world resumed its motion. She smiled and lifted her dull, wet eyes to him.

She said, "Trick or treat."

ON THE NIGHT OF THE FUNERAL, LEE DECIDED TO sleep at home. Moira drove him because she wanted to pick up a pint of ice cream. She sped through the slick streets, riffling through a box of cassettes with one hand. They could've been years in the past, stealing away from Russell to find a bar or camp on Bird Island, or to skip everything and go straight to bed. The familiarity relieved and vexed him. There was a tingling along his nerves, a building anticipation, as if she were driving him into an undiscovered country. Along Ocean Drive, the bay looked like petroleum and the sprawling homes were still strung with Christmas lights. Luminarias lit one sidewalk; Moira had once told him how she used to kick them over on Christmas Eve.

She tossed the cassettes in the backseat. She'd found nothing. "Who needs a sound track?"

"Not us," he said.

They stopped at a traffic signal. The glow of the red light tinted Moira's face. She said, "Actually, I fucked a man in Amsterdam. At that swingers' club. Was that obvious at the table?"

"No," he said. He blew into his hands. The engine idled, a loose screw vibrated in the dash. He expected the signal to turn green, but it didn't, and he saw her under the tube lights, under the faceless man. "No, you fooled us."

She nodded distractedly. The light stayed red, but the road was abandoned and after a moment, she accelerated through the intersection.

"I didn't intend to," she said. "He just had such, I don't know, *certainty*. Mostly I remember his skin tasting metallic; he probably worked with steel. Not really my type, but who knows, maybe we loved each other for a few minutes."

"We would have to know what love is to know that," Lee said. The words sounded confident and mysterious, even romantic, which he liked, though he'd never considered them before. He spoke differently around Moira, always had.

She parked behind his mother's Olds and cut the ignition. The headlights stayed beaming on the bumper and a single streetlamp distinguished the small houses of the neighborhood. She said, "You're sure you don't want ice cream?"

"I'm fine." After saying this, he wondered why he'd answered that way.

Rain drummed on the hood, streaked and pilled the windows. As he reached for the door, she said, "It must have been a nightmare."

For days, those words had hovered in conversations but no one had said them straight out. They made him feel caught in a lie. Moira bit her lip. In the dimness, she looked forlorn and exhausted, years older than she was. He felt sorry for her and suddenly longed to console her. He almost admitted that every time he'd seen his mother's car since her death, and even when she was still breathing but dull-eyed and relegated to the hospital bed, the words *She's home* scrolled through his mind. He heard them, even envisioned the letters, and his heart stuttered. The words had come when he came from Russell's to dress for the funeral, when they had returned to the house afterward. *She's home. She's home.* He considered telling Moira that the words had come just moments earlier when she steered into the driveway and killed the engine.

He said nothing. If he'd spoken, he would have wept, and leaning across the seat, he realized weeping terrified him. Moira no longer reeked of incense, but he smelled her perfume, maybe the same musky scent a woman had worn that morning, maybe one his mother had stocked when she sold Avon. At first her mouth stayed tight, and for an extended, desperate moment he feared she would recoil and push him away. But soon she touched his face and let him taste the wine on her tongue, let him breathe her warm breath. She moaned, a soft whimpering that made him self-conscious, like a teenager worried his parents were spying through a window; the moaning exhilarated him, too. Moira's jacket rustled when he pulled her closer. He pressed his face to her neck; he inhaled her. He listened to her breathing, to her voice saying, *Take me inside*; he listened to the cars on the road, to their tires hissing like fireworks before they explode into light.

"WHAT'S THE CRUELEST THING YOU'VE EVER DONE?" Moira had asked years before. They were parked just outside the fence at Cabaniss Field, at the end of the runway, watching planes practice touch-and-go landings. They had been together for a few months, and lately she'd been posing such questions.

She especially liked to ask them after they made love— Have you ever *really* broken someone's heart? What's the blackest lie you've told? What's your most depraved fantasy?— then because the questioning seemed to give her such a charge, they usually rolled around again. He'd never answered in earnest, afraid what he had to offer would betray his inexperience; at twenty-six, he had no secrets worth keeping. Nor had he ever gathered the courage to turn the questions back on Moira, knowing that at twenty-two, she had plenty.

The lights of a single-engine turboprop appeared in the sky, descending toward the landing strip.

"Or, no, what's the cruelest thing you *would* do?"

"Depends."

"Would you hurt someone if he didn't deserve it?"

"Of course not."

"What if I asked you to? Or your mother did?"

"You wouldn't. She wouldn't."

"Say we did. Say we wanted you to really hurt someone, and the only reason we wanted you to was to prove that you would."

The plane grew nearer, a darker patch of dark in the charcoal sky. His mother was home, watching the Lifetime Network.

"Yes," he said, "I would."

Moira fixed her eyes on the runway, smiling slyly, obliquely. She reached across the seat, found his hand and pulled it to her lap. At first he thought she'd taken hold of him because he'd snowed her into believing he was capable of that which he wasn't; now, her tightening grip, her slightly sweating palm, even the lights on the plane's wings, showed she didn't believe a single lie he'd told.

A week later, walking in Heritage Park, she told him she was leaving, that there was someone else.

"Who?" he asked.

"I don't know yet."

A WEEK AFTER CHRISTMAS, LEE FOUND HIS MOTHER gasping short, high-pitched breaths. He'd fallen asleep on the couch in the den, and when he woke he switched on a lamp, expecting to see her crying. She wasn't. Her eyes were glazed and bleary, fixed on the ceiling. He checked the oxygen tubes for kinks, adjusted the cannula in her nose. He ran warm water over a washcloth, then blotted her forehead. He wiped her cheeks and limp, listless arms. He asked her to squeeze his hand or blink, but she stayed still, her breathing sharp as blades.

At four in the morning, their hospice nurse, a stout Mexican man named Tony, answered after just one ring. Tejano music played in the background. Lee detailed his mother's day; soggy cereal for lunch and two diaper changes; she had slept most of the afternoon and evening but was current on her pills; the catheter bag was half full; he could not remember the last time she had spoken. Tony asked him to lower the phone so he could hear her breathing. Lee held the receiver close to his mother's mouth and wondered how long she had been in this condition. He wondered if she'd called for him while he slept.

A coma, or similar to one. Her lungs, Tony said, were filling with fluid that had leaked through the membranes, a result of protein depletion. He said lungs are like sponges and when saturated, air cannot penetrate them. He said he'd expected this—Lee realized Tony had turned off the Tejano music— and was surprised it hadn't happened sooner. In the den, her ventilator whirred. On the phone a distant nighttime static buzzed. Tony apologized.

He told Lee to place a morphine tablet under his mother's tongue and dissolve it with water from a straw. The pill would relax her, take pressure off her lungs, though soon her breathing would likely slow to such a degree that it would completely cease. Her body was shutting down. Tony said he was coming over, but he lived across the bay in Portland, so the drive would take half an hour. Lee told his mother not to worry and turned on the television because he didn't want her to feel alone while he went to the kitchen. He found the pills and poured water into a glass. He took one of the crazy straws that she liked and returned to the den. He smiled in case she could see.

He spoke to his mother as if she were a child. He pried her mouth open while her eyes stared vacantly forward. Her tongue was pasty, rigid. Her breath smelled oniony. Her jaws clenched, making a muffled chewing noise. When he held them open, the high-pitched breathing became a strained groaning. He relented. He closed his eyes, forced himself to breathe. *Please,* he thought, *please.* After a moment, he opened her mouth again. She bit him. Then again. Then he lifted her tongue, held it awkwardly with his finger, and positioned the tablet. He leaned over to suck water into the straw, then trapped it with his thumb on the top. Once released into her mouth, the water dribbled down her chin and drained into her throat. Liquid gurgled in her chest. Her body coughed. Then she lay still. Lee opened her mouth and saw the tablet, still dry. He drew water into the straw again, set it directly on top of the tablet and watched its edges effervesce. He climbed into the bed. Through all of this, he talked to her. Tony had said, "Let her know you're there. She can hear you, and she's scared."

He complimented her and he lied; he spoke of his father, because, suddenly, he understood she'd want to hear of him. He recalled for her the months his father had spent beneath his old Subaru, reversing the transmission's gear configuration just to see if it would work; the time they had tubed down the Frio River and the current kept pulling him into the weeds so that finally he followed them on the far bank; his singsong way of answering the phone. Lee spoke calmly, and hearing his voice, he realized his mother's life was ending in these very moments. He turned off the television. He put his arm around her shoulder, cradled the fragility of her bone, flesh. He asked her questions, then answered them. When he ran out of things to say, he cleared his throat and began singing.

He sang "Amazing Grace" in a near-whisper, like a lullaby. Her teeth began to grind and she started groaning again. Her head lolled, her fingers twitched. Her dry, peeling lips lost color. Lee sang louder, ashamed to realize his voice had a sudden, pleasing resonance, a warm reverberation buoying his tone. He started and abandoned and returned to different verses without thinking. The harsh, labored panting began to taper. He kept singing. He did not let his voice waver, but concentrated on maintaining a clean, even pitch, for slipping off-key seemed unpardonable. His mother's breathing calmed further. He sang, sang, sang. And when her lungs finally and quietly gave in, when her fingers went still and her jaw relaxed, he kept singing as he pulled the quilt to her shoulders and closed her eyes with his hand. He stayed beside her while the world started rushing away. He plummeted through an opening emptiness, his body surrendering as if the earth and gravity were receding. He floated through nights on Russell's couch and through the funeral, and he kept floating until he landed in his bed with Moira.

The rain came harder as he moved inside her. She straddled him, and he touched her eyelids, her mouth, neck, breasts. Her skin was milk-blue in the night. He fought to remember each time they'd made love before, entrusted her to envelop and consume him, like the rain outside, like the ocean, to make him feel as she had years earlier, to say his name and remind him who he was.

Moira held his face with her warm, trembling hands. She said, "It's okay."

She draped her arm and leg across his body. Headlights from a line of cars cut through the window of Lee's room, then she rolled onto her back and said, "Ice cream turns my stomach."

"Not your average pillow talk."

"I wanted to drive you. I didn't want you to be alone." She sat up, bunched the sheets around her. Her hair shone as she stared out the window. Lee felt his heart beating. She said, "Maybe I made a mistake. Do you wish this hadn't happened?"

"I kept thinking of you. When it was happening, I couldn't stop." Just as he said this, as he wished he hadn't said anything, he realized it was true. Holding his mother, when he owed her his strictest attention as he owed her his life itself, he'd been unable to keep Moira at bay. Just on the other side of the moment, she was biting her bottom lip, playing pool; she was dousing her eggs with Tabasco sauce; she carried a baker's rack down the stairs when Russell moved into his apartment, carried it because they'd said she couldn't; she was tussling with him in the mornings, teaching him the beauty of occasional sexual stillness, and he was resting his cheek on her stomach afterward. As soon as she had come to Lee years earlier—he'd never been so deluded to think he'd pursued and caught her—he'd started waiting for her to leave. When his mother was dying, his heart had leapt because he knew Moira would come back.

She ran her fingers through her hair. He caressed her flesh, the curvature of her ribs and the space between the bones, then he let his hand fall to the bed. A torrent of memories swirled: how, massaging his mother's back, he'd always waited for the first moment she kindly said he could stop; how after he'd taken her for a Demerol injection at the ER, she'd blissfully said, "From now on, I'm going to do better"; how before the local tremors took over her hands, she'd been delighted for days by crayons and coloring books. Now he felt wistfully desperate, as he had when Moira had been prone to asking her grave questions. What would she ask tonight? He imagined his furtively beautiful answers, imagined them arousing her and delivering the two of them into another sweating tangle of limbs. More than anything, he wanted another chance. Below his longing was a whirling disgust for having spoken of his mother, for drawing the comparison that would remind Moira of the night's gravity and rekindle, whether by guilt or kindness, the ruthless passion he so desired.

She climbed on top of him again, placed her hands above his shoulders. Sweat glazed her skin. She said, "I'm so sorry."

He smiled and raised himself to kiss her. She let him, but that was all. She draped her hair behind her ears, then lowered to her elbows and began stroking his face, peering at him in the near-dark. Again she whispered, "I'm sorry." She pressed her cheek to his, then lay beside him; her body relaxed. Years before, in Heritage Park, when she had claimed to both love him and no longer love him, when he begged her to stay and knew she wouldn't, he'd felt the same dread. He listened to her easy breathing, listened until it quieted. On her hip, he felt a tiny half-moon of raised flesh. Possibly the scar had been there for years and his greedy fingers had never noticed it, but he suspected the wound was more recent, the consequence of a mundane miscalculation, a timely slip on wet pavement or a hard pivot into an open kitchen drawer. Such a small thing, but it intimated the trajectory of Moira's coming life: Soon she would be working in an office, a dour job to help with a mortgage; she'd be married to a kindly, complacent man; she'd be pregnant. If she remembered this night, the memory would be fleetingly sad—a last example of who she thought she'd become; Lee's presence was arbitrary. He knew this as surely as he knew she'd be gone before sunrise. Her lungs filled and emptied with air, and when she was immersed in the steady rhythm of sleep, he crept out of the room.

The den still stank of cigarettes and old talcum. The odor hollowed him, turned his ankles to puddles. Moonlight slanted through the blinds; the rain had stopped. He lay in her hospital bed, naked and shivering, and covered himself with her quilt that smelled of the petroleum jelly he'd rubbed on her cracked lips. He had the distinct sensation of being borne toward a cliff. His thoughts went not to his mother—each memory of her seemed as irretrievable as a half-forgotten dream—but to the women at the funeral, to Russell, and to Moira, for suddenly—keenly, terribly—what they had understood all along became clear: This was only the beginning. Nothing would estrange him from the rootlessness ahead. Fits of sobbing would seize him when he least expected, in traffic and the shower, in the grocery and two years later, in his St. Louis classroom—and tonight, as he clutched the bed's guardrails and clung to the red tinsel his mother had never seen. He would hold on too long. Then, he was swept over the edge and weeping for all of them, weeping like a man who was dying or a newborn child, blind and terrified and gasping for breath.

———

HIS MOTHER HAD SOAKED IN A BATH AFTER THEY returned from Mexico. When she stepped into the den, she smelled of soap and steam. She situated herself in the recliner and said, "I'm sorry I got upset in the car. Maybe I drank too many margaritas, but they were so good."

He lay on the couch, watching the late news. The Santa piñata stood atop the television. He said, "Water under the bridge."

"Did you talk to Russell? Did he have a nice holiday?"

He nodded, though he hadn't spoken with him at all. Russell would have asked about their trip, about her health and spirits, and Lee would have been obligated to contrive hopeful, winsome answers. Tonight he lacked the energy for such condolences.

"Don't appease me," she said, unwrapping a pack of cigarettes, "but I'd like to hear what you remember about the old holidays. That's fair on Christmas." She blew a plume of smoke into the air. "Don't tell me about sneaking into your presents. We knew about that."

"You did?"

"Don't ever become a thief. You don't hide things very well," she said. "Tell me something else. I won't get upset."

Immediately, as if he'd been awaiting the opportunity, he said, "I used to lie awake, listening to you and Dad set out the gifts. You always wanted them arranged a certain way."

She laughed a little laugh, then stayed smiling. "I did, I did."

"I'd wait until you had everything perfect, then pretend to wake up. I made noise to warn you."

She turned to the window, the tip of her cigarette glowed orange when she inhaled. A wave of guilt swamped him. Maybe all of their Christmases blurred and conflated in her mind, but more probably she remembered what he hadn't mentioned, what in his fatigue he'd not thought to avoid. On at least one of those mild December mornings—though over the years he suspected it was their annual tradition—she and his father had made love after arranging the presents. From his room, Lee had heard their muffled voices in the hall, heard their bedroom door easing closed and bodies sinking into a mattress. After they opened gifts, his parents shared cigarettes. His childhood seemed a haze of bluish smoke. He could not recall what his mother had looked like then, though he could imagine her as a child, opening her own gifts. She was a wistful girl who would never want college or money, just a husband to care for her, a child she could care for. Maybe tonight she felt she'd wanted too much.

"You have a good memory," she said. "I do, too. It's not always a blessing."

"No," he said, "I guess not."

She stubbed out her cigarette, then lay back in the recliner. She said, "I'm sorry you're going to remember all of this, all of what's coming. It's not fair."

By rote, he began, "We just need to—"

"Don't say anything, Lee," she interrupted. "I'm okay tonight. I'm optimistic."

She pulled up the quilt, raised her knees so her feet rested on the cushion. She was trying to keep her eyes open, and though he wanted to encourage her before she drifted off, to thank and exalt her, he said nothing. Ever so slightly his heart had started to cave in and render him silent. When he looked again, her eyes were lidded and she was breathing peacefully; he lowered the volume on the television, so she wouldn't wake. If the night could relieve them of the day, he believed the morning would find him rejuvenated, replenished.

"Maybe optimistic is wrong," she said, suddenly awake. "Maybe tomorrow I'll be gloomy, but I think we'll survive this. Next Christmas, we'll drink margaritas in Mexico. You can bring Russell, maybe that little sister of his if she's here, and this will all seem like a bad dream. Won't that be nice?"

He couldn't answer. Her lighter snapped, the fragrance of smoke wafted. He sensed her staring at him, but closed his eyes and stayed quiet. As his mother waited for his familiar, reassuring voice, he rolled over and pretended to sleep.

BRET ANTHONY JOHNSTON's fiction has been featured in *The Paris Review* and *Open City*, as well as many anthologies, including *New Stories from the South: The Year's Best, 2003* and *2004; Prize Stories: The O. Henry Prize Stories 2002;* and *Scribner's Best of the Fiction Workshops 1999.* A graduate of the Iowa Writers' Workshop, where he received a teaching-writing fellowship, he teaches creative writing at California State University, San Bernardino, and can be reached online at www.bretanthonyjohnston.com.